The Escape R

Plus ça change, plus c'est la même chose.
- *Jean-Baptiste Alphonse Karr*

Copyright

First Published 2019.

Copyright © Sean T. Rassleagh, 2019.

The moral right of Sean T. Rassleagh to be identified as the author of this work has been asserted.

The Escape Room is a work of fiction.

All rights reserved.

Starters

Friday, July 1, 2039.

Sheriff Cockburn always enjoyed sentencing day in the Court for Historical Crimes and Grievances. The prosecution spared no expense to ensure a guilty verdict so almost every case ended in sentencing. Evidence was provided by video and over the last six weeks in his packed courtroom, the prosecution had been premiering one-hour episodes of their mini-series 'The Crimes of Clan Campbell', culminating with drone footage of a hundred extras re-enacting the massacre of the MacDonalds in Glencoe. After the viewing by the jury, the programmes were immediately released on all major streaming services and watched by millions all over the world. As the scene of women and children dying in the snow faded the procurer fiscal had demanded the death penalty.

The defence, by contrast, had come up with a disappointing thirty minute poorly edited documentary shot on someone's phone. The sheriff was annoyed: the production values of the defence case were unacceptable. Of course, both the online poll and the jury in the courtroom had come down conclusively in favour of guilty. The defendant was the current clan chief of the Campbells and under the Historical Crimes Act held responsible for the crimes of his ancestors as well as his own crimes as the owner of Argyll Lettings the largest landowner in the city. An ideal villain for the court to throw the book at on prime TV.

The great thing about the Historical Crimes and Grievances Court as daytime TV drama was it imposed punishments from the time of the original crime. The court had great latitude in applying historic practices because of its location in Edinburgh's Old Town: a historic area recognised by the United Nations. Period costume was required for everyone attending court and the historic courtroom was a worthy backdrop for the drama that would unfold. After the guilty verdict, the defence had asked for four hundred additional crimes and misdemeanours currently on file to be taken into account. The sentence was bound to be severe.

Naturally, Mr Campbell was far too important and rich to appear in court himself. He had nominated an actor to take his place as the sentence was read.

The sheriff straightened his judicial robe, cleared his throat and placed the black cap over his powdered wig at five pm exactly. There was immediate silence in the packed courtroom. The camera zoomed in for a close-up as the sentence was pronounced.

"Archibald Tolleymacher Campell, it is the sentence of this court that you are to be draggit behind a horse from the Tollbooth to the Mercat Cross and there you shall be broken on the wheel and hung by the neck, you shall be castrated, your bowels shall be spilled into boiling oil, and your body sawn into quarters, your head shall be mounted on a spike at the Netherbow and may the Lord have mercy on your miserable soul." The sheriff pronounced the dialect word 'draggit' with especial relish: it was the little period touches which added to the authenticity of the show.

The sheriff paused. The good bit was over: now came the compromise which had allowed the act establishing these show trials to pass through parliament.

"In the alternative, a fine of ten thousand Euro payable to the court clerk within one hour. These proceedings are closed." He banged his gavel.

"All rise!" shouted the bailiff and the sheriff left the courtroom.

People said the historic crimes trials were a mere show for the tourists because the fines allowed were so small and credit was available to those with no cash on hand. The sheriff recognised the entertainment value but also thought it was cathartic for society to bring historic wrongs to light and show people that even death and the space of several hundred years could not thwart justice. He had passed many death sentences in his time on the court, ordered floggings, burnings and drownings but in every case, the defendant had paid the fine and walked away intact.

Down at the bottom of the Royal Mile in Holyrood Palace, Archibald Campbell stuffed his face with more popcorn and turned from the TV screen to his solicitor.

"Well, that didn't go too badly. So what's the damage again?"

"It's costing us five thousand euros. Your substitute offered to go through with the execution for half the price of the fine. He's not that bright."

The landlord chuckled and grabbed another handful of popcorn. "I've never seen anyone get hung, drawn and quartered before. It should be fun."

The TV channel had gone back live to the courtroom when they realised that in half an hour the option to pay a fine would be gone. A local historian was informing the presenter that unless the fine was paid the actor would be the first person facing public execution in Scotland since the notorious Ratho Murderer was hanged in 1864 and that the actor's execution, if it happened, would also take place in Parliament Square.

As time passed the actor looked remarkably self-assured for someone in his position. Seeing that nobody had appeared to pay the fine officers in the red jackets of the town militia and carrying halberds had surrounded the dock, making sure he could not make a run for it. There were only fifteen minutes left to the deadline when he stood up in the dock.

"Fetch the sheriff, I wish to make a confession."

The landlord hadn't expected that. His pudgy hand grabbed more popcorn and he sat up - in as much as was practical for someone of his grossly obese frame - in rapt attention to the new development.

There was commotion in the court. The bailiff called for silence and the sheriff was hurriedly summoned back from his chambers.

"Your Honour, I wish to confess to fraud. My contract with Archibald Campbell was entered into using a false name and forged signature. The contract is invalid!"

"And what is your true name?"

"My name is Donald MacDonald of Glencoe!"

There was uproar in the court.

The sheriff banged his gavel for order.

The court clock struck six.

Sheriff Cockburn asked for a copy of the actor's contract and read it with care. He called the learned advocates for prosecution and defence to approach the bench and make submissions. Then he announced his decision.

"The time allowed for payment of the fine is now expired. Mr MacDonald will be held in custody pending investigation of his claim that his contract is invalid. Should the contract be found invalid Archibald Tolleymacher Campbell does not have a contracted substitute and will, therefore, be subjected to the sentence himself. Mr Campbell is ordered placed under house arrest. Mr MacDonald, you will be prosecuted for contract fraud should your contract prove invalid and executed in Mr Campbell's place if it is upheld. The court will reconvene once the investigation into possible contract fraud is concluded."

— ♦ —

Monday, July 4, 2039.

Chief Constable Robert Merilees' phone buzzed on the bedside table. He was lying in bed with his wives in their double-upper flat in Springvalley Gardens. His first wife, Margaret, groaned and put her pillow over her head. "Not again. Do you really need to bring that thing to bed?" His second wife, Jessica, was closest to the bedside table and she reached out and handed him the phone.

He was old enough to remember when the people of Morningside would have raised an eyebrow at his domestic arrangements. But property prices had been growing faster than incomes for so long that two adults living together could rarely afford a house or flat. As soon as polygamy was legalised three and four-person marriages became common. Even if you were well off like Margaret and himself a third salary meant you could afford something nicer without stretching to meet the rent at the end of the month. Hardly anybody could afford to buy property in Edinburgh any more: you either inherited it or you rented.

The gender identity laws allowed people to identify as whichever gender they chose and change their minds whenever they liked. There were no paper documents or plastic cards any more so changing gender identification was as simple as flipping a setting on your phone. Many people had taken one male and one female first name to make it easier to exercise this right. The minister at their church didn't like it at all but the chief constable wasn't bothered. All he knew was he had a nice house and two wives: one male and one female both younger than him. No fifty-five-year-old man deserved a forty-year-old female wife and a thirty-two-year-old male wife. Life was good. The biggest problem he had with the new laws was keeping track of pronouns. It wasn't easy to remember when to say 'he' or 'she' when your genetically female wife occasionally liked to identify as a man and your genetically male wife identified as female at home and male at work.

The phone had buzzed because he had a new e-mail from Professor Hume, one of the senior advisers to the Scottish Government. They'd met quite often at official engagements and had many of the same friends. It was an invitation to a party at the professor's house: a farewell party. The chief constable was shocked to learn that the professor had health issues and he and his wife had decided to be euthanised. This would be their leaving dinner and guests would be welcome to take any small items from the house. They had no children and they wanted their friends to have their things.

He showed the e-mail to Jessica. His second wife was a detective inspector he'd met at work and she was more interested in the politics of his career than Margaret. Margaret had her own career and earned even more than he did.

"You need to go Bobby, and you should take Margaret instead of me, she will fit in better with that crowd. Bring back something nice for the house, I heard the professor has a library of real paper books."

Margaret had woken up and started to pay attention at the words 'dinner party'.

"Dinner parties are so boring since they banned farming animals" she complained "but there's bound to be some nice stuff in the professor's house. They're so rich and his wife has exquisite taste. We have to go! I'll wear my new dress."

So it was settled, The chief constable e-mailed his condolences and said he and his wife would be honoured to attend Professor Hume's leaving do.

Taking Margaret was the right decision, Jessica was too young to fit in with the bigwigs in the Professor's social circle. Margaret would do a much better job of socialising: no doubt she had met many of them professionally. Jessica took his phone and put it back on the bedside table for him. She snuggled into him and wrapped his arm over her chest. He licked her earlobe. She pulled him closer.

"Do you two never stop?!" complained Margaret "well, be quick if you have to. I need my sleep." She rolled over and turned her back to them.

It wasn't long since the chief constable had taken his second wife and the two of them were still making love several times a day. Soon enough it would be twice a week like with Margaret, so better enjoy it while he could. He reached down and pulled up the hem of Jessica's nightdress. Soon the bed was shaking, they couldn't help it.

"Right!" said Margaret, angrily. "That's it!"

Chief Constable Merilees sighed. Sometimes he wished he could sleep with his wives one at a time but they had agreed they needed a home office more than a second bedroom so it had to be three in a bed.

In the morning it was time for work. Jessica woke up first and went to shower. She only identified as a woman at home with Bobby and Margaret. When it was time for work she'd be Duncan again, her female name reduced to an initial. Detective Inspector Duncan J. Chisholm of the Recent Crime Division.

"Darling, I have to stay late at the brothel this evening," said Margaret, looking at her phone.

"OK dear, are you staying over in a cell?"

"Depends how late I run. I'll probably be finished early enough to come home. I'll text you!"

She was nearly ready to leave for work now, tapping on her phone to summon a car. Dressed in a conservative, expensively tailored dark-blue knee length skirt and jacket. A tasteful slit over one knee showing just a little thigh. And on her lapel a small gold pin instead of the usual plastic staff badges: 'H.M. Brothel Edinburgh. Ms Margaret Noyce, Madame.' Mrs Noyce-Merilees used her maiden name at work and she insisted on the French spelling of her job title. She found that, when correctly pronounced, 'Madame' was suitably respectful, but cosmopolitan where the English 'Madam' sounded harsh and almost vulgar and 'Governor' was simply banal and authoritarian. Madame Noyce was in charge of what was once Edinburgh's prison.

— ♦ —

Tuesday, July 5th, 2039, 11.30am.

James Miranda Fergusson rolled out of bed. He took a few steps across the room to the fridge and got himself an Irn Bru and a large packet of paprika crips for breakfast. His laptop was still running the code from last night, it hadn't crashed yet, which was a very good sign. He'd gone to bed about five am after pulling yet another all-nighter. This project was killing him. But it was fascinating and combined his two favourite things: playing video games and neuro-electronic interfacing. Mostly playing video games. He looked out the window of his top floor student room. On the other side of Holyrood Road and along to the left he could see the offices of the company that produced the game, lit up in red for the launch of this year's edition: the fifteenth. Beyond that Salisbury Crags loomed through the haar. The company had two long-running game franchises. One about stealing cars and driving fast around a city and one set in the Wild West. James Fergusson thought the idea of stealing cars and driving them yourself was silly: cars were things you summoned with your phone, told them where to go and let them get on with it. The Western game was more fun so he was putting all his effort into that.

After he scraped a 2.2 in Computer Engineering and Biology his supervisor had recommended that he applied for the PhD program. She steered him towards a research assistant position funded jointly by the video game company and a biotech company that had spun out from the department and made the MedChips that the NHS used to monitor and medicate all its patients. He was to research human-computer interfaces for total immersion in the virtual world of the game. His supervisor was Dr Roberta Knox-Hume the designer of the original neuro-interface chip which had been used in medical applications for many years. His part in the project was to write the code to interface the game servers to a player with the implanted electronics. To do it right he clearly had to become an expert player and that required a lot of selfless dedication. He'd get right back on it after breakfast.

There were four new e-mails on his phone and another paper letter under his door. His MedChip reckoned he needed to get more exercise, a lot more exercise. Maybe even go outside from time to time. And cut down on the cola and snacks. What did it know? Why didn't it just dial up the insulin and blood pressure meds and stop bugging him? He had code to write and the whole of the Wild West to explore.

He decided he needed to pee and as long as he was walking over to his tiny en-suite bathroom he figured he may as well pick up the quaint old paper letter that had come through his letterbox. He wondered why they even put letterboxes on doors these days. He tore it open. Shit! It was from the court. He'd been reported for his bad eating habits and lack of exercise. Damn MedChip. The Ecological and Health Crimes Division of Police Scotland had issued a 100 euro ticket for causing excess financial risk to the NHS. Payable immediately. He chucked it on his desk, put his massive over-the-ear headphones back on and flipped the virtual reality visor down to cover his eyes as well, completely shutting himself off from the sights and sounds of the real world. He'd worry about the ticket later: right now he had to get back on his horse. There was a bank to rob.

James Fergusson was not the greatest computer scientist in the world. He wasn't even in the top ten. The Guild did not mind that because they had more than enough brainpower of their own. If he wanted to play video games all day that wasn't a problem either, as long as he was not too worried about the finer points of the law. They needed somebody who wasn't going to object to a little experimentation on themselves from time to time and wouldn't mind helping them acquire raw materials for their experiments. Someone who wasn't squeamish about the messier aspects of human experimentation. Most importantly, they needed someone who could be disowned if things went wrong. Because the brain-interfacing chip work had the same problem now as it had had since its inception twenty-five years ago. Finding enough brains.

— ♦ —

Friday, July 8, 2039, 5 am.

Ten miles south of Edinburgh at the edge of the Pentland Hills, a well maintained single track road led off the A702. It wound through arable fields and vegetable gardens until, just before a large reservoir, it arrived at a hamlet. The laird's house and a cluster of cottages around it for estate workers and family friends. Everyone living here was working for the estate one way or another. No strangers. Just past the manor house the road narrowed and crossed a small river. A wrought-iron gate barred access to the bridge and a concealed security camera watched for anyone trying to circumvent it. There was a small sign "Harthill Farm. Finest Organic Milk and Semen. A carbon-negative facility." with a number to phone for access across the bridge. A second sign warned walkers "Warning. Pentland Hills Predator Reintroduction Program. Wolves, lynx and bears have been introduced to this area. Access beyond the barrier fence is at your own risk."

After the high fence along the river bank, the road wound through a small plantation. Dense trees blocked the view of what lay beyond from anyone on the other side of the river. A kilometre further there was a second gate at the entrance to the farm. Then the road passed through fields up to the farmhouse itself and the surrounding barns.

The setting was idyllic, a stream running down from the hills, the carefully restored old farmhouse and the manicured lawn and gravel turning circle in front of it. Everything spoke of money, the drive well surfaced with no frost damage or potholes, the barbed-wire on the fences shiny and new, the house newly painted. The quiet hum of the electric wire behind each of the fences.

Jean Dickson was already awake when the sun rose at five am. She was older than she looked, managing the family farm for many years now since she had retired from the university. She liked being her own boss and the rural life and she liked to be up before dawn. It was completely dark at the farm, the nearest streetlight miles away and on a clear night, you could see thousands of stars. She had her telescope in front of the open window of her bedroom and was looking at Mars today. The bright red planet, our closest neighbour after the moon. When she'd been a child she'd wanted to be an astronaut and go to Mars, but the more practical career option of veterinary science beckoned and she'd spent her professional life as a researcher a few miles away at the Bush Estate campus of the university.

Today was going to be a busy day. New stock was arriving this morning and one of her oldest animals would be moving on. She'd grown attached to her but that was farming life: the livestock were there for a purpose and there was no point in being sentimental. She lived on her own in the farmhouse now, a few stockmen and a cook came down from the hamlet in the morning to help with the daily tasks. She hadn't given up on science in retirement, she had her lab in the basement of one of the barns and a few personal projects, just to keep her hand in.

It was sometimes lonely, she remembered the times ten years ago when her young niece would come down from the big house to play on the farm during the school holidays. She'd had a black Labrador when her niece was young. Her niece had called it 'labradog' and spent hours with it. Those had been good times, but her niece grew up and left to go to university, she'd completed her degree and the last she heard she'd been apprenticed. It was probably for the best that she made her own way.

Things were different on the farm from when her niece had played there. Fifteen years ago she had run sheep on the hill and cattle in the pasture. These days farming animals was banned: the carbon cost per calorie of human food produced was just too high. So was keeping dogs as pets. But other opportunities had arisen, like the grant from the EU for rewilding the hills. The farm was powered by a small hydroelectric turbine on the stream and a few wind turbines on the hill. It produced far more electricity than was required for its own needs allowing the operation to claim carbon-negative status. With farming of animals banned and a wealthy city close by the market for human milk and semen was booming. The rich were not willing to do without natural dairy products entirely - no matter how much they cost - and there were always debtors whether it be from student loans, rents or court fines ready to sign away a year or two of their life and live in the spartan circumstances of a negative-carbon facility in return for payments towards their debt and free accommodation. People in the herds on the farm had the legal status of farm animals and it was easier to refer to them as if they were horses or cows. Humanising them just made it difficult if they had to be slaughtered: but she tried to treat them well. As long as you stayed healthy and productive life on her farm could be pleasant. Apart from the induction of course. Fresh, healthy food, plenty of exercise, outdoors much of the time and no stress or work to perform beyond donating milk or semen three times a day. Since the farm was carbon-negative it was exempt from the population control laws: she could breed from her cattle without requiring a licence for each pregnancy as long as the offspring never left the farm. She was running nearly a hundred head of human cattle now in her ten fields and five barns.

Today she would be saying goodbye to one of her favourite cows. She'd grown up on the farm, born nineteen years ago. She looked like she'd be a good milker but she hadn't been clipped and she wasn't milked with the dairy herd although she ran with them in the field. The farm was being paid to stable her by the owner, and now the owner had sent for her. She'd be loaded up this afternoon, the instructions were delivery to the slaughterhouse before five pm. A pity. But there were ten new beasts arriving this morning from the court. Life went on.

Cock au Van

Friday, July 8, 2039.

As one would expect Professor Hume and his wife, Dr Roberta Knox-Hume, had spared no expense on their leaving dinner. Academic colleagues and leading lights of the Edinburgh political and business establishment were arriving at his elegant three story townhouse in Rankeillor Street. Each of them experiencing a little frisson of fear when they saw the black van parked outside, not wanting to look but unable to help themselves. The professor and his wife were waiting at the door to greet their guests. Behind them the lounge was already filling up, guests chatting and sipping wine. Upstairs, a few of the academics were examining the volumes in the professor's library. The table in the dining room was already laid and preparations well in hand in the kitchen. Waiting staff and a prominent chef had been hired from a Michelin starred restaurant to cater the event.

Everyone had arrived and the professor mingled with his guests, making sure to have a few words with all of them. Anticipation gradually grew in the room as time passed and the smell of cooking vegetables wafted in from the kitchen. Everybody was excited: dining out had become a relatively rare occurrence since the raft of emergency laws designed to mitigate global warming. Farming of animals for food production was banned because of the huge greenhouse gas emissions from meat production relative to vegetables and cereals. Everyone on the planet - outside of rogue states like England - had been forced to become vegetarian. In Scotland, many people were now living off balanced nutritional powders supplied by the NHS. Just add water to a few scoops of powder three times a day to cover your calculated nutritional requirements. Food was arguably healthier than before but without animal ingredients like milk, butter, eggs and meat much of the pleasure of dining out had been lost.

One of the waitresses entered and caught the attention of the professor's wife.

"Chef is ready for you now, madam."

She smiled at her guests and followed the waitress out of the room. The conversation paused for a minute and then picked up again. Tension palpable in the air.

A few minutes later the chef himself knocked respectfully on the door of the lounge and caught the professor's eye.

"I'm ready for you, sir…"

Standing just behind him at the door were two men wearing leather aprons.

The professor finished the last of his wine and walked to the door. Dead silence in the room.

As he crossed the threshold the two assistants took their station one step behind him. The dining room was on the left and the kitchen a few steps further down the hall but the men in the aprons led him to a small study while the chef returned to his pots.

"Professor, please take off your clothes. All of them please."

Trembling slightly the professor took off his clothing, watch, wedding ring and shoes.

" and, I'm sorry, but we will need to tag you "

One of the men clipped a plastic tag with a digital QR code to the professor's ear with an industrial tool. It hung there like a large earring. While he was distracted the other man buckled leather cuffs around both ankles. Swift and practised it took them only a few seconds. The point of no return had been passed.

"That's it then… come with us…."

They were holding his arms now, one on each side. They opened the door to the kitchen. The smell of roasting vegetables filled the air. In front of them was a large polished copper container like an old-fashioned bath. And above the bath his wife hung naked and upside-down, suspended from a metal beam by the chain attached to the cuffs around her ankles. Blood still trickled from the gaping wound in her neck into the copper tub.

The professor looked at his wife's pallid body and smiled. Everything was going to plan.

"Kneel"

The professor knelt in front of the bath. One of the men grabbed his hair and pulled his head up. The other swiftly drew a large knife which had been concealed in a scabbard behind his back and slit the professor's throat. Blood spurted out and they held him still to make sure it landed in the copper bath, mixing with that already collected from his wife. Once the flow subsided sufficiently they clipped the cuffs around his ankles to chains and hoisted him over the bath. He hung next to his wife, twitching for a few seconds while the last of his life drained into the tub. Once the professor's body was still the slaughterman took a picture, making sure the tag in his ear with the official code authorising slaughter for human consumption was visible. An app on their phone connected to the server at the register of deaths and the data was written to the blockchain, marking the official time of death. All the necessary assisted-suicide consent forms had been submitted by the professor and his wife. The death was recorded as voluntary the meat was certified as legal for consumption.

Only a few years previously what had just happened would have earned everyone involved life in prison but in the midst of the climate change and over-population crisis, the professor's gesture was regarded as generous and ecologically sound.

The man with the knife sliced carefully through the professor's neck and removed his head. His colleague opened a red plastic box. Trails of smoke-like condensation formed as the damp air of the kitchen met the super-cold interior of the box. The cooks studiously looked in the other direction as the head was placed in the box. The professor's wife had already been beheaded and her head safely stowed in a second insulated box while they were waiting for his corpse to stop dripping. The first slaughterman snapped the lid shut, picked up both boxes and left through the back door. Preserving the heads was the first illegal act of the evening.

The man with the knife began dismembering the professor's wife as she hung suspended over the bath. As the breasts and each arm and leg was removed they were passed straight to the cooks to be washed and seasoned. The professor and his wife had left detailed instructions about what was to be served to each guest, right down to the particularly unpleasant colleague who was to be presented with his anal sphincter. The team worked quickly and efficiently. While the guests were enjoying their soup course the steaks were already on the grill. The professor's genitals were sliced off and prepared as a chef's special for a guest of honour. His wife's breasts a delicacy for another special guest. Some of the collected blood was used to make gravy, the rest mixed with flour to make black pudding. The organs and unused meat ground up with spices to make sausages. Nothing was wasted. When they were finished the kitchen was meticulously cleaned and the bones and few remaining scraps of the bodies tossed in a black garbage bag to be taken back to the slaughterhouse for cremation.

The dinner had been a great success. In the absence of the hosts, toasts were made in their honour. Over coffee and liqueurs the company spoke with admiration of the skill of the chef and how the professor had bravely insisted on halal slaughter, foregoing stunning to ensure the best tasting meat. As they left the staff offered the guests gift-wrapped portions of black pudding and sausages to take with them.

Meanwhile the hosts' heads, safely in their coolers and submerged in nutrient solution were on the front seat of the black slaughterhouse van. The seatbelt carefully passed through the handles of the coolers and clipped in. No chances were being taken The van had been instructed to travel at the highest allowable speed. Time was of the essence but this was not the first time the slaughterman had done this run. Everything would be waiting for his arrival.

— ♦ —

Friday, July 8, 2039. 10pm.

The black panel van turned off the A71 and into the yard behind a small industrial estate. Sandwiched between two food preparation businesses, the slaughterhouse loading dock was identified only by the unit number: five. The slaughterman got out, looked up at the CCTV camera beside the loading dock and waved. A second later the facial recognition software identified him, the metal shutter started to rise and he reversed in. The shutter closed behind him. He picked up the two cases from his front seat and stepped out. He was in a large, two story high, steel framed shed with a smooth concrete floor. Along one side of the building space had been partitioned off from the industrial floor with drywall. An office for the manager and then a larger space, completely sealed with its own air-conditioning unit which maintained the air pressure inside at a slightly higher level than outside. If the seal was broken then air would flow from inside to outside and no contaminants would enter the clean area.

He opened the metal door into the clean space and entered quickly shutting it behind him to make the seal again. In front of him, in the entrance area was a low bench, to the left a set of lockers for outdoor clothing and on the right fresh clean-room coveralls and a shower cubicle. To enter the clean area you took off your outdoor clothes, showered and picked up a clean room suit. You sat on the bench to put on the clean room suit - no part of the suit or the clean room clogs could touch the floor on the dirty side. When you had it on swung your legs over to the clean side. But the slaughterman wasn't crossing into the clean area, everything beyond the entrance vestibule was well beyond his pay grade. The slaughterhouse manager, Helen McDougal, was waiting on the clean side for the two cases. He placed them on the bench and left. She wiped down the outside of the cases carefully and waited for the air pressure to stabilise after the outside door closed. Then she opened the inner door.

Everything beyond the second set of doors was polished and sterile. In the first room a girl of about twenty, wearing only a hospital gown was strapped to an operating table. Her head was shaved and life support and anaesthetic machines stood ready at the side of the table but not yet in use. In the second room, an intensive care bed waited for the patient to recover after surgery. The third room was different: it had several waist height steel-cased industrial machines, more like what you would see in a silicon chip factory than a hospital and in one corner a ceiling-high rack of computers. The manager opened the lid on the first machine and placed Professor Hume's head on the robotic stage, closed the lid and pressed the large green button. The robots would take it from here.

Clamps moved in from either side and screws drilled into the professor's jawbone making sure the skull was held absolutely firmly. A robot arm selected the first tool and the preparation began with shaving the skull. A CT scanner formed a detailed three-dimensional image and the computers started to work out the sequence of cuts to excise the professor's hippocampus. The table rotated the skull in the X, Y and Z dimensions as the cutting plan was put into action. The machines with their multiple robotic tools were far faster than human surgeons and far more accurate. Scraps of bone and tissue began to fall away from the professor's head into the base of the work area. From time to time cutting stopped so the debris could be flushed away from the surfaces being worked on with a water spray. In the bottom of the work area a garbage disposal unit ground it up and flushed it into the waste pipe. It only took a few minutes before the hippocampus was collected by the robotic arm and placed on a steel surgical dish. The light on the front of the machine turned green and the completion of its task was announced with a metallic 'Ting'.

The manager waited until the anaesthetic took effect and the patient was asleep before wheeling the robotic surgical unit over to the operating table and clamping it down on the floor. Patients were less trouble if they didn't see the robotic arms, saws and scalpels. The procedure was programmed into the machines, they'd taken the CT scan to plan the surgery earlier. This surgery was more delicate than that on the professor's head because they expected the girl to survive and return to full health afterwards. The manager knew nothing about the surgery, she'd only been trained on which machines to put where. When she was done she said, "Computer: start brain surgery protocol 23 B." In a few minutes, she'd need to fetch the professor's hippocampus from the other room. Then she'd load the professor's wife's skull into one of the other preparation machines. Half an hour after that the robotic surgeons would be finished with the girl on the operating table and she'd need to move the patient into the recovery room and attach the ICU equipment. If things went well the girl would get up in a few weeks. If they didn't go well she'd be processed in the slaughterhouse like their other customers. Either way, the manager would be paid for her evening's work.

The robotic surgeon was seeking out the hippocampus in the girl's brain based on the 3D CT scan data that had been collected earlier that day, it was going to cut it out, spray a special gel to foster neural growth in the cavity and then place the hippocampus from the professor in the empty space. A partial brain transplant. The technique was first carried out successfully on mice more than fifty years earlier but this procedure was much more sophisticated. This was Guild technology. There would be no problem with rejection because the girl on the operating table had identical DNA to the professor - except for XX rather than XY chromosomes and a few minor enhancements suggested by his doctors. She was a clone, created twenty years before using a slightly edited version of the professor's DNA and now old enough to fulfil her function. Her body would provide him with another thirty years of youth and health. Professor Hume fully expected to live several lifetimes and had decided it was only sensible to experience life as both genders. It would be an interesting experiment and it wasn't a big risk: he'd already put in the order for this clone's replacement and it was a boy. If the female body wasn't working out he could swap back to a male body as soon as the new clone was old enough to accept the transplant.

Neurons would grow to connect the brain material together, just as they had done in those mice fifty years ago. Now it was just a case of closing up the skull: the robots bonded the bones and closed the wounds with a special photo-sensitive mesh activated with a laser rather than old-fashioned sutures. When her hair had grown back there would be no visible trace of the surgery. She was brought from the operating table to the ICU bed attached to monitoring equipment and given infusions to keep her unconscious while she healed. A catheter drained her bladder as she slept. It would be three weeks before she would wake.

— ♦ —

Saturday, July 9, 2039.

Detective Inspector Chisolm was back at his desk on Saturday morning, working on the Guild file. The prime suspect had died so the file needed to be updated, and because this was off-the-books and not part of his official caseload he had to do the work at the weekend. The first entry in the police file on the Guild was now forty years old, a brief handwritten note from a Detective Sergeant in Lothian and Borders Police on a conversation he had overheard in Deacon Brodie's pub in the Royal Mile in 1999. A group of seven university professors were conspiring to form a secret society to advance scientific progress more quickly by pursuing research on human cloning without regard for the law or scientific ethics.

Lothian and Borders Police was long gone now, subsumed into Police Scotland. The Guild file was assigned to the Recent Crimes Division, but it was not kept on the police computer and there was no record of it at all on the official filing system. Over the years investigators had noticed that records related to the Guild on the computer were often subtly different from what they remembered writing and that if they made a note about a line of enquiry evidence started to disappear. They suspected the Guild had sources within the police and access to the police computer. Eventually, extreme counter-surveillance precautions were taken: only the chief constable and the officer assigned to investigate it knew about the Guild file. Any new entries were handwritten in an old-fashioned A4 notebook and kept in a decades-old safe with a mechanical lock.

Detective Inspector Chisolm turned to his computer and searched the deaths database. He found the paperwork for Professor Hume and his wife Dr Roberta Knox-Hume. All the forms completed correctly a few days before and notarised by their lawyer, even though that was not strictly required. Deaths were certified by their euthanasia provider and the photographs left no doubt the subjects were deceased. The tags in their ears matched the rest of the paperwork: the meat was authorised for consumption. The bodies were completely gone, cooked and eaten, nothing left for forensics to look at. He turned to social media and used his official login to get access to everything that had been posted about the party last night whether or not the posts were public. Several guests had been Instagramming pictures of their plates, meat on the menu was a rarity even for the rich. Involuntarily his mouth started to water when he saw the steaks, it was so long since he had tasted meat and the chef had done an outstanding job. Visually each plate was an artwork with the meat as the centrepiece flanked by vegetables and colourful sauces. Margaret had posted a picture of her plate. A long, cylindrical cut of grilled meat flanked by two meatballs and a dab of white horseradish positioned just above and to the left. Not a particularly subtle final message. Detective Inspector Chisolm wondered if the professor was aware of his investigation and the message on Margaret's plate was intended for him.

Suspect deceased: case closed. That happened a lot in these investigations. Too often to be a coincidence. Whenever there was a case where Guild involvement was suspected somebody died. Usually a witness, occasionally the investigating officer and sometimes the suspect but there was never any evidence of foul play. He was sure the Guild was a large organisation with many different illegal activities. Professor Hume's file was closed but it wouldn't be long before there was another Guild case. He put the notebook in his safe along with the ones from previous cases and locked it. He made a note on his paper to-do list with a date three weeks into the future "Check who's been looking at the social media on the party". A long shot.

Another thought occurred to him. He brought up the paperwork on the death again and noted down the name of the company which had carried out the euthanasia. If the professor trusted them that much they might have links to the Guild. He'd just been assigned an apprentice police constable, maybe he could use some of her time to look into them, even though it wasn't strictly speaking an official investigation he could put it down as training.

— ♦ —

Friday, July 29, 2039.

Three weeks later and the girl was out of the ICU bed. The drips were gone, there was still a monitor checking her vital signs, but it clipped to her hospital gown and she could move about. Her new life was not pleasant: pain from the surgery, nausea from the drugs, weakness from being bedridden for three weeks, blinding headaches and nightmares. But she was sure it would get better. Slowly, it did. Within a few days she was strong enough to be moved back to the farm to convalesce. This time she had a private room in the farmhouse, not a stall in the barn. She could walk outside and watch the herd of human cattle in the field. Lure them to the fence with an offer of chocolate so as to pet them. The professor knew two of them well: the mare who was pregnant with his new clone and the stallion cloned from his wife's DNA. Their original plan had been for Roberta's hippocampus to be transferred into her clone and for them to have a second married life, this time as wife and man, in the two younger bodies, but Roberta had chosen another path. Maybe Roberta was right and a new life was time for a completely different adventure.

Over the years they had visited the farm together many times to see their clones. Life on the farm agreed with the clones - healthy food and plenty of exercise, no worries about school or work. There was no point in schooling a brain whose memory centre was going to be cut out and discarded. Physically they were near perfect specimens, naked when they ran in the field in summer and genetically enhanced in the key areas. And now the professor's consciousness was in the young mare's body and the stallion cloned from his wife's DNA was nibbling chocolate from her hand. Her headache had been gone since yesterday. The stomach cramps she'd had for a few days were gone too. She felt great and as she looked at the naked stallion she was becoming aroused.

Professor Hume noted the unfamiliar sensations with curiosity and excitement. There was so much to learn about this new body. She was discovering it wasn't just a new body, it was a new mind too. Only the hippocampus in this brain had come from her old self. She had the professor's memory and sense of self, but all the rest of the brain belonged to the clone. She now had the eyesight and reflexes of a young woman but she had lost the practiced skill of the professor in programming or solving mathematical equations. The clone was female and had lived its entire life stress free on the farm, it had never lied, or cheated or fought for anything or worked hard to solve a mathematical problem. While the conscious voice inside the professor's head still thought of 'I' as a sixty-year-old man her subconscious brain reacted as a carefree nineteen year old woman. A nineteen year old woman who was seriously attracted to the stallion she'd been watching in the neighbouring field for years.

The farmer, walked over to chat, the farm dog, a surprisingly small black Labrador running ahead of her to sniff the professor. Many years ago the professor and Dr Dickson had been close friends and colleagues but they had drifted apart since she'd retired to her farm.

"I thought pet dogs had been banned," said the professor, mildly annoyed by her indiscretion. Guild members were supposed to appear to be upstanding citizens. But the farmer had always pushed the limits even when she worked at the university.

She smiled. "Dogs are banned, but cats aren't. A cat is carbon-negative because it reduces food wastage by eating mice. Brodie is a labracat."

The labracat heard its name, stopped sniffing the professor, stretched and jumped easily onto the fence post next to the farmer. The farmer scratched its head and it purred and wagged its tail.

The professor decided it was better not to say anything even though the farmer had clearly engineered a brand new species just to get round a bye-law about keeping pets. There was no point in getting angry. Dr Dickson was a founder member of the Guild, their original expert on cloning, and had more than enough Guilders to do as she pleased. And anyway, the stallion cloned from Roberta's DNA was far more interesting.

"The two of you need to get a room," said the farmer, "why don't you use a stall in the barn. He's always lived in the barn, he won't want to go in the house."

The professor's conscious mind was appalled at the suggestion but her subconscious mind wasn't and her subconscious mind had control of the hormones. The clone had been in the field with this herd her entire life and had seen the other mares taken to the stall in the barn to be mated or implanted with cloned embryos.

There was a lump in her throat. "OK…"

The professor led the stallion to the barn and when they were finished they fell asleep side by side on the straw.

As she slept the stallion's sperm were swimming hard towards the egg which had just implanted itself in her womb. An egg which shouldn't have been there at all. By law the NHS configured women's MedChips to prevent conception unless they had purchased a licence to reproduce, but that law didn't apply to human cattle on a farm. The slaughterhouse manager should have changed her MedChip from the settings for livestock to those for humans before she left. But she hadn't. A new batch of customers had arrived and the manager was upstairs in the reception area when the professor had been collected.

— ♦ —

The surgery involved in the first part of the professor's plan had been dangerous enough. The second part was even riskier but just as necessary.

She now had a cloned body, forty years younger than the old one and a different gender. Her DNA was not exactly the same as that of the original professor but close. If the new body was DNA tested they probably wouldn't even bother to match against male samples, never mind samples from dead people and if they did the match would not be exact. With a small amount of luck if for some reason her new DNA was run against the police database it would not connect her to the professor. Her assumption was that at some point in the next few years enough of the professor's activities would come to light that being connected to him by the police would be a bad thing.

However, having DNA which didn't match the professor was not enough. Her DNA wouldn't match anyone at all, there was no registered person on any government system with this DNA. Illegal clones don't have their birth registered. She was a non-person. No school records, no exam results, no job, no flat, no family. She could hack the computers and create those things but that was not a good starting point for what she hoped would be a long and successful stay in this body. Nobody would remember her and if someone looked into her background properly her story would fall apart. She still had her Guilders which allowed her to purchase Guild technologies and services and a number of other cryptocurrencies. She had spent many hours training herself to memorise the secret keys to access her cryptocurrency: all she'd need to do so was a PC with a secure internet connection and the right software. What she needed now was an identity she could live in for forty years.

It had to be a girl of roughly the same age and roughly the same physical shape. Small discrepancies could be explained or dealt with surgically. It needed to be someone qualified to attend university - some of her happiest memories were of life as a student and she wanted to go back and do it again. Someone without strong family ties and few or no friends. Ideally someone with a respectable social background and ideally someone who was physically attractive. She didn't want to swap the face of this perfect clone for something worse. That is what would be required: she was going to have to get the face, hair and eyes of another girl. The hair was important: if she was ever required to give a DNA sample she could give hair and it would match her new identity and the DNA of her assumed family. The eyes were needed because people remembered eye colour and so many things were tied to iris scans these days. Getting a new face and eyes meant more surgery and it meant someone was going to have to die.

She had a few weeks to get used to her new gender and new body before then. Her clone's subconscious feelings could be trusted about life on the farm, but the clone didn't know anything about life as a woman in the city. She had never walked in heels or used makeup and had no social skills. Even thinking of herself as 'she' instead of 'he' was difficult for the professor after decades of being 'he', but she needed to get used to it or she was bound to slip up.

She would leave the farm at the start of the university term. Just another undergraduate fresher in fresher's week when nobody knew anyone. The professor wasn't interested in conventional wealth or power, she'd had those for the last twenty years. She'd intentionally left her house, possessions and all but a thousand euros of her fiat money behind. She wanted to be a new person and experience youth again, including the inconveniences. She wanted to study something different, maybe slack off and have a social life but most importantly she wanted the thing which was missing from her previous life: children. Not immediately of course! Once she had enjoyed her second youth. Maybe when she was thirty or thirty-five.

Unfortunately for Professor Hume, the semen from his wife's clone was of excellent quality and it wasn't going to take nearly that long.

— ♦ —

Thursday, September 1, 2039.

Victoria Alexandra Campbell shouldered her rucksack, picked up her suitcase and walked down the stairs from the first floor flat on Atholl Road she'd called home for all her eighteen years. Her mother was working in the shop below but she didn't stop to say goodbye. They'd said all that needed saying last night. Her bags were heavy but Pitlochry is a small town, it was only a short distance to Station Road and the train which would bring her to university in Edinburgh. Her student loan had come through, flowed into her bank account and straight back out again to pay for tuition and a tiny room in a student hall. The term didn't start for another month, going down early would mean she'd have to find an extra month's rent but it was better than staying at home another day. Maybe she'd get a job waitressing: whatever happened she'd get by.

She'd never met her father but she knew she'd been given his surname despite him not being married to her mother. Until yesterday evening her mother had refused to talk about him or how she'd lost her job on the big estate. Her mother had opened their shop with her termination payment but after a few years the lease had been bought out by the House of Bullkitsch conglomerate and they had become employees rather than owners.

The House of Bullkitsch had started out as the operator of the only public convenience on the A9 between Perth and Inverness. With a canny head for business, they saw opportunity in the line of desperate tourists and hillwalkers which snaked around their parking lot. Gradually their facility was extended until the half-kilometre queue for the toilets was entirely enclosed within the largest tartantat emporium in the Highlands. Their most lucrative niche was the new New Georgian middle class who had driven north in their Range Rovers to view the King's holiday home just up the road at Balmoral and now wished to dress like the proprietors of a Highland estate.

However, even the best business ideas don't last forever and as time passed the volume of urine flowing into the faux-baronial bogs off the A9 started to dwindle. The train was once again the mode of transport of choice for tourists visiting the Highlands: private car ownership had been superceded by self-driving electric cars summoned with a phone. The House of Bullkitsch moved with the times and began to buy up all the tourist shops near the station in Pitlochry and along the Royal Mile in Edinburgh. Many small shops with different names on the outside but the same tat on the inside. Victoria's mother's little shop was called 'The Royal McNab', it catered for the offspring of the New Georgians. You could buy miniature crossbows with quivers, skinning knives and spring-traps for little Nigel along with the requisite Harris Tweed jacket and cap, tartan trews and brogues. For his sister, there were Barbour jackets, pink pinafores, pink Hunter wellingtons, stuffed toys of adorable Beatrix Potter characters and wooden dollhouses with real gaslights and fireplaces. Hidden away in the back room, they had a small collection of golliwogs and unredacted copies of Tintin and Huckleberry Finn for the racist grandparent market.

Victoria had often wondered about the name of their shop. 'The Royal McNab' sounded more appropriate for a pub than a gift shop. Her mother would only say the name had been written into the agreement under which her previous employer had paid the start-up costs for the business and there was a non-disclosure clause with a massive financial penalty if she said more to anyone. Yesterday, Victoria had typed the shop name into Google to see what would come up. An article on an upmarket estate-agent website explained everything.

"Scottish country sportsmen dream of achieving a 'McNab' - catching a salmon, shooting a brace of grouse and stalking a stag in the same day. And if you sleep with the housekeeper it's a 'Royal McNab.'"

After an hour of tears and recriminations, her mother had told the truth. She'd lost her job as the housekeeper of the big sporting estate after a guest had booked their Royal McNab package. For a mere 10,000 euros, success was guaranteed along with a parchment certificate signed by his lordship to commemorate the achievement. A team of ghillies was on hand to deal with any problems encountered in the salmon, grouse and stag aspects of the challenge while a family pack of viagra and an antique gynaecological couch once used by Henry VIII ensured even morbidly obese guests could complete the final part. The problem, in this case, was that the guest had said nothing when the condom slipped off his preternaturally petite penis: Victoria was the result. That guest had been Archibald Campbell, back in the days where he was still thin enough to get about in his sedan chair.

As she stared from the window of the train across the Forth towards the EU naval base at Rosyth, Victoria's determination to go against her mother's wishes hardened. She'd read about Archibald Campbell's death sentence on a news website. When she got to Edinburgh she was going to visit him before it was too late. Her father couldn't be as bad as everyone said and if he was rich enough to buy Holyrood Palace surely he would help out with his daughter's tuition fees.

Cold Cuts

Saturday, October 1, 2039.

The professor arrived in Edinburgh Waverly International by steam train on a warm and sunny Autumn day. Edinburgh often had better weather at this time of year than in mid-summer. She'd been driven to the station in Penicuik by the farmer, taken the train south for a few stops, then got off and taken the next train back to Edinburgh. Nobody should be able to make a connection between the clone left at the station by the farmer and the new identity she would assume. The train which brought her to Edinburgh was an international service which had come all the way from London. At the EU border just north of Carlisle, the train had been stopped, passports had been checked and any undocumented refugees arrested. Only steam trains ran through England these days: when England exited from the United Nations in order to 'take back control' and avoid the climate laws the sanctions had made it difficult to keep more advanced locomotives running. Steam was the only option. The New Georgian ruling class in England thought their steam trains were wonderful: English ingenuity at work.

As she stepped down from the train she could see the passengers queuing up next to the airlock doors on the adjacent platform. The hyperloop to Glasgow, Belfast and Dublin was getting ready to depart. The service was packed today: the Edinburgh Festival was winding down and tourists were returning home.

The station was underground now, but you couldn't tell that from within: the old glass roof had been replaced with a concrete plinth onto which an image of the sky as it would have been seen through the original roof was projected. Above the plinth rose the McLeod Caledonian Tower and Casino: a sprawling hotel and conference centre topped with a tower rising sixty stories into the air The top three floors of the tower, capped by the trademark Basil Spence monopitch roof, harling stonework and varnished timber panels required by the planning regulations were higher than either Calton Hill or

Arthur's Seat. With views to match, they had been taken by the building's lead tenant: the Court of Oracles.

The lower fifty-seven floors had brought thousands of new low-cost hotel rooms to the city. Instead of windows, the low-cost rooms had computer displays showing what the view would have been: the screens were so realistic there was no way for the customers to tell the difference between them and a window that couldn't be opened. The lower floors couldn't have windows because they were surrounded by a thick layer of metamaterial. Light hitting the tower refracted within the metamaterial and emerged from the other side as if it had passed straight through the building. All that was visible of the sixty-story structure when you looked from the Old Town towards the Forth was the top three floors. The visual impact planning regulations for new buildings in the old town specified a maximum height of three stories with a Basil Spence roof and sensitively chosen materials but nobody had thought to say that the three stories couldn't be floating, apparently unsupported, fifty-seven stories in the air.

As she walked across the station towards the canal which ran along its eastern side the professor had nothing in the world but her memories, the comfortable walking boots and outdoor clothing she was wearing, a thousand euros in cash and one very specific additional garment she'd asked the farmer to procure for her: a balaclava. Of course, her memories included the 512-bit secret keys that would unlock enough cryptocurrency to buy the whole city, twice over. But her cryptocurrency wasn't going to help without a safe place to work, a computer, a secure internet connection and an identity.

Her main problem was CCTV cameras. They were everywhere and all networked together into the police server. In the centre of town image recognition software was continuously matching every face against the massive police database and tracing people as they walked from camera to camera. Almost every person would have a known identity. A few would be wanted and the system would inform any police officers in the area. And a few would be unknown: not matched to any face on the system. Unknown was not illegal but it was interesting. A tourist might not be identified until their biometric passport data was uploaded or they spent some money and identification came in from a bank. The longer you walked about unidentified the more likely the AI algorithms analysing the images would send someone to stop you and ask for identification. An illegal clone that had been brought up on a farm and never registered with any state organisation would be unidentified for sure.

The professor headed towards the Market Street exit from the station and turned right on the canal towpath towards the Nor'Loch. This part of town had changed radically over the last twenty years. The city needed new infrastructure to deal with the flooding that was becoming a regular occurrence as a result of climate change. Rainfall was forty per cent higher than at the start of the century but the real problem was when a storm brought a week of continuous heavy rain. The solution had been to deepen and extend the old Union Canal so it could function as a storm drain and to allow the western half of Princes Street Gardens to flood, restoring the Nor'Loch. When intense rain was forecasted the Nor'Loch and canal were partially drained providing the capacity to capture large quantities of water and then discharge it slowly to avoid flooding. As she approached the canal tunnel under the Mound she took the balaclava out of her pocket and pulled it on, A few minutes later she saw the brightly painted Bryce Cruises narrowboat 'Isabelle' approaching as arranged. The narrowboat steered close to the bank, only a foot from the towpath, matching her pace. Her contact had put small chalk tick marks on the path to mark the dead zone between CCTV cameras, once she was safely out of view of the cameras she jumped on board and went immediately through the hatch and under cover.

She was in a pleasant lounge area. A middle-aged lady in a neatly cut business skirt-suit sat on a sofa on one side of the narrowboat. Coffee and biscuits were ready to serve on the table in the middle of the cabin. She sat across the table from her host on the sofa which ran along the other side of the boat.

"Good afternoon, madam. Everything is ready when a suitable donor becomes available, until then I've prepared my office for you to stay in."

"Thank you. I'm sure everything will be satisfactory. To be clear, there are no cameras on this boat or in your office?"

"Of course not."

"Very well. If there were cameras now would be the time to tell me: there are severe penalty clauses in the contract..."

"There are none."

Drinking coffee wasn't easy when wearing her balaclava, a straw would have been handy, but she got the hang of it eventually. The important thing was the manager did not recognise her as the clone she had transplanted the professor's hippocampus into. When she got her new face there must be no trail back to the professor.

The narrowboat was powered by an electric motor: it was almost silent and moved slowly. No more than walking pace, across the Nor'Loch under the shadow of the castle. The railway lines were now enclosed, under an embankment at the side of the Loch. There was a kiosk where kayaks and rowing boats could be rented and a queue of tourists eager to part with their cash on this sunny autumn day. The Ross Fountain now rose from the middle of the Loch on an artificial island and children were clambering carefully from their rented boats onto it to paddle in the clean fountain water. The narrowboat nosed into the long tunnel which would take them to the lock at Fountainbridge where they would join the original Union Canal.

The old canal had been deepened but was otherwise much the same as when it had opened in 1790. Expensive modern waterfront flats and restaurants beside the lock and the mooring basin gave on to a pleasant stretch with joggers and cyclists on the towpath as they passed parks, older tenements and student halls. Then through the leafy suburb of Craiglockhart, past the rowing club boathouse and over an aqueduct. Eventually, nearer the edge of the city, the surroundings became less prosperous and more industrial. The boat steered towards the edge of the canal on the opposite side from the towpath and tied up to mooring rings on a wall which formed the boundary of a loading yard behind some industrial units, leaving a little slack in the ropes. The towpath was quiet here, the sort of place you would think twice about walking by yourself after dark.

The helmsman came back into the body of the boat. She recognised the man who had slit her throat a couple of months before. She half wanted to thank him for the fast and almost painless job, but she said nothing. He opened the door which led from the lounge area into a small galley and pressed a concealed button under one of the galley units. The section of the floor he was standing on smoothly descended beneath the waterline. The bottom of the narrowboat had been extended with a plexiglass underwater viewing area which ran most of the length of the boat and had its own set of manoeuvring controls. Even though the canal was deeper and the water was purer now than in the past - there were fish and even otters in some of the more rural stretches - a glass-bottomed tourist boat would be quite a novelty on the Union Canal. But this was no tourist boat. Instead of seats, there were metal rings on the floor for fastening chains and the ceiling was covered in thick acoustic tiles. Unwilling guests in this section of the boat could scream as much as they liked. Nobody would hear.

The helmsman walked over to a small panel, finished in brass in keeping with the restored narrowboat and scanned his iris, switching the steering controls to this location.

"Set condition one throughout the boat! Prepare to dive!" The helmsman couldn't help himself: he always had to say that.

The manager sighed. "Boys with toys."

The professor smiled and pretended to agree. But secretly she thoroughly approved of the helmsman's announcement. In her previous life, she had spent considerable time and effort to design and build this boat and it felt fitting she was making this journey to a new life on it. The boat's current task of moving people and equipment unseen by the ubiquitous CCTV was not the first, or the most important, service it had performed for the Guild. Many of the advanced systems the boat had carried during the struggle for Scottish independence had been removed as they were unnecessary for its current mundane role.

The boat started to pump water from the canal into its ballast tanks and slowly slipped lower in the water. Only a foot or two was needed. Next to the control station on the side of the boat, well under the water line was a docking port. The helmsman nudged the boat forward slightly lining it up with the matching structure, invisible under the water on the wall of the canal and gently applied lateral thrust to bring them together. The docking structure on the boat mated with the matching structure on the land side with a click and bolts spun tightening the metal port against rubber gaskets until a watertight seal was formed. A green light came on and the helmsman opened the hatch on the boat and then the second hatch on the land side. They walked out into a wide concrete pipe. The pipe rose gradually from the underwater entry port, under the loading yard and into the space beneath one of the industrial units where it ended at an elevator.

There was no button for the floor they were on in the panel inside the elevator and no 'down' button in the panel on the floor above. As far as anyone using the elevator to get between the floors of the building above would know this basement level did not exist. They went up one level and emerged onto the slaughterhouse floor.

The manager's office was next to the rooms with the surgical machines. The professor knew the setup perfectly, after all, it was her Guilders that had paid for it. Her severed head had been operated on by those machines only a few weeks ago, although obviously she'd not been conscious at the time and had no memory of it. The manager had provided a sleeping bag on the couch in her office. The window on the office was fitted with privacy glass - she could see out but nobody could see in. Perfect. And now she would wait.

The university had grown and grown over the years. There were now almost a hundred thousand students. A substantial fraction of the population of the town. Maybe ten thousand new freshers starting this week. In a new town for the first time. Probably feeling lonely, maybe a little inadequate, worried about the debt they were about to incur, worried if they could keep up with the coursework. Some of them were sure to feel depressed, maybe even suicidal. But even so, the odds of someone suitable using the slaughterhouse's assisted suicide service by chance in the next few days were slim. The manager didn't believe in leaving things to chance.

Every year, the slaughterhouse gave a generous donation from their marketing budget to a mental health hotline for students. The manager was a volunteer counsellor and had made sure that female freshers at the University who called that week would be passed over to her. She'd offer to meet them in person. A cup of tea and a friendly chat. If they matched the requirement a few drops of the right pharmaceutical in their tea and a version of the slaughterhouse leaflet which gave the number of a particularly sympathetic doctor. Then let things take their course. Just a little nudge.

It took three days, waiting in the office, watching the monitor showing the new customers entering reception. Searching the internet for background information on any girls whose face looked like it might fit. Finally, a girl the manager had talked to a few days before came in. The professor zoomed in on her face. She was perfect: Victoria Campbell, a freshman student in English Literature and Law. About as far from the professor's previous career as you could get. She had a pretty face, her height was right and her skin was a good match to the clone's. The professor pulled on her balaclava and left the office. The manager was waiting expectantly.

"Yes, she'll do."

— ♦ —

Monday, October 3, 2039, 5 pm.

Apprentice Constable Justine Claverhouse knew she had been lucky in her life so far. She'd been brought up in the countryside south of Edinburgh and educated at Biggar Academy. When she was eighteen, against the wishes of her parents, she'd moved to the city to attend the university. She'd completed her undergraduate degree in law, an MSc in criminology, a postgraduate diploma in forensics and a two-year internship with Police Scotland. And now she'd been selected for an apprenticeship with Detective Inspector Chisholm of the Recent Crimes Division. If she did well in just a few more years she might become a full-time constable and be paid a salary. Of course, as an apprentice, she still had to complete a few more modules at the university which would mean more debt added to her student loan. But, with a bit of luck, she would manage to complete her training with less than a quarter million euros of debt and she'd have an actual paying job at the end of it. Which was far more than most of her generation: much of the work people used to do was now done by machines. Even work that was skilled and beyond the present ability of computers such as writing software or creating content for websites was often 'open source' and unpaid. The only businesses that were prospering these days were renting houses and collecting interest on loans.

Last year interest and repayments had started to be due on her first student loan. She had no income to pay them and no intention of asking her parents for help so she quickly fell behind and began to be issued tickets for defaulting on her debt. Domestic service was one of the very few paying jobs still available. Of course, her salary would be seized to pay off the interest on her debt so she wouldn't actually get any money: but at least she'd have free accommodation and no ticket to pay every week. There were robots to do the housework: these days the point of having domestic servants was to demonstrate the employer's superiority and social status rather than to carry out the actual chores. In New Georgian society, the fashion for the gentry was to have uniformed staff to do their every bidding and interact with technology for them. Using a computer or cellular phone or anything from the twenty-first century themselves was beneath a New Georgian gentleman or lady.

She had found a position in the household of an American visiting professor in the English department at the university. It was a one year contract as a chamber maid in exchange for accommodation in a small bedroom within their flat and her master making the interest payments on her debt. Her mistress, Dr Claire Streatham, was also an academic: Assistant Professor of Intelligent Design and Dance at the Christian University of Minnesota and a prolific author of wizard-related fan-fiction.

When her master and mistress had guests she had to wear her uniform and wait on them at table. Otherwise, she just had to attend to the housework and provide sexual favours as required. The contract had the standard corporal punishment clause but the professor and his wife never invoked it and rarely asked for more than the occasional blowjob and that she shared their marital bed for a threesome on Fridays. Even better the additional academic qualifications required for the chambermaid job were minimal. She'd only needed to purchase one semester worth of training at the university where she'd learned about waiting table, how to show appropriate deference to her master and mistress and the correct etiquette when receiving traditional forms of discipline. All in all, as far as jobs went, this was definitely a keeper.

What was even better was the room that came with it. For decades the university had been acquiring property all over Edinburgh as it relentlessly expanded and used the income from student fees to buy more buildings rather than pay adequate salaries to its staff. Why pay staff properly when so many people were willing to do academic research for a pittance? Every year there was a new crop of students with doctorates looking for a career in academia. Five years ago the university had outdone itself and bought Edinburgh Castle from the army. The castle had been converted into a residence for the vice chancellor. The castle vaults which once held prisoners of war now accommodated his extensive wine cellar. After purchasing the castle the obvious next step was to buy the adjacent Ramsay Gardens and convert it into grace-and-favour apartments for senior staff and visiting academics. As the maid her bedroom was a former linen closet within one of the ornamental turrets: but even the linen closet in an 18th-century apartment was bigger than her previous room in the student flats. At some point in the past, a tiny window had been installed. When she lay on her bed she could see the statue of a cat which graced the roof of the neighbouring apartment, peering over the edge onto the gardens on the hillside far below. If she went over to her window and put her head out she had a stunning view over the Nor'Loch and the New Town to the Forth.

Today she was in a rush, walking back to Ramsay Gardens from police headquarters at St. Leonard's, through the university's George Square campus and past the student flat where she had lived as an undergraduate. She was on Alex Salmond Bridge, passing the Police Scotland Division of Historic Crimes and Grievances which occupied the former City Library and National Library buildings, heading toward the Royal Mile, the true centre of power in the town. The streets and lanes around the Royal Mile formed the National Historic Area: cars and robots were banned from public view for several hours a day, the LED street lights were programmed to flicker like gaslights and recently the New Georgian administration in the City Council had agreed that residents should be given a discount on their local taxes if they agreed to wear historic dress. At the top of the Royal Mile was the Castle and the university administration. At the bottom, Holyrood Palace, the townhouse of Archibald Campbell, owner of Argyll Lettings and Chairman of the Landowner's Alliance. In the middle, looking out over the New Town from the Mound, the official residence of the Governor of the National Bank of Scotland. Not that the Governor was there very often. These days, he preferred his country estate, off the Carrefour Bancquier in the French Quarter by the airport.

She got to the junction of Alex Salmond bridge and the Mile. She would usually turn left to return home to Ramsay Gardens and order the evening meal. Only the extremely wealthy could afford space in their apartment for a kitchen these days: it was far less expensive to order from an automated restaurant. One of the inconveniences of living in the historic area is that delivery by drone was not allowed, so she'd have to go and collect it on foot when it was ready. But before that, she had an errand. To her right were the law courts, St Giles and the Council Chambers. Straight ahead, on the other side of the junction from Deacon Brodie's Pub the historic building containing the Procurer Fiscal's office, the Historic Crimes Court and the Central Ticket Unit: her destination Her pulse started to rise as she pushed open the swing door.

As a police officer, she knew the place well. She crossed straight to the Ticket Office and went to the desk. Sergeant McTear was on duty.

"Hello sergeant, I've come to pay a ticket for my mistress, Dr Claire Streatham."

The sergeant typed the name into his computer.

"Hi Justine, yes, I see it. That's a class two ecological infringement from this morning. She was caught by a plainclothes officer at Starbucks putting the wrapping from her cake in the orange recycling bin instead of the brown one. Oh....yeah.... and there's another one coming up from last month. Hurtful speech on social media. She called someone an idiot on Facebook. Are you paying that one as well?"

Shit. She hadn't said she'd got outstanding tickets. "I suppose so...."

"Well that's a class two and a class three misdemeanour so a total of five points. Sixty euro a point so a three hundred euro fine or five hours unpaid sex work or six strokes. What's your poison, Justine?"

"May as well get it over with. I'll take the strokes."

"Fair enough. Just go through, the bank has bought the corporal punishment rights for today. Corporate entertainment."

He tapped the corporal punishment option on his screen and a few seconds later her phone vibrated in her pocket. That was the MedChip App notifying her that pain control for her hands and buttocks had been temporarily suspended under a court order. Usually, the MedChip would automatically block out any continuous pain and reduce the intensity of any sudden pain. It didn't block pain entirely because it was important to know if you'd hurt yourself and to have an incentive to seek treatment if you were unwell. There was also a limit to what it could do - severe pain still needed drugs to control - but it effectively controlled day-to-day discomforts like headaches and tried to minimise pain if you were injured. Every week the MedChip received a new database of viruses and made sure your immune system would recognise and deal with them. For someone who'd had a MedChip implanted as a child, pain was something of a novelty. Even respectable people, when faced with the choice between a fine and the punishment booths, sometimes opted for the booths out of curiosity. At least the first time.

"Can you check if Sheriff Cockburn is available. Tell him it's me."

The sergeant picked up the phone on his desk and spoke briefly.

"He says he'll be free in a few minutes, you can wait here, don't join the queue."

There were four punishment booths in operation for females and a short queue of miscreants waiting. She could hear the sound of a strap whacking against flesh from the booth on the right and soon the malefactor emerged cupping her hands under her armpits. She gave Justine a wry smile as she walked past. Comrades in adversity.

"Booth 4," announced the sergeant.

The woman at the top of the line shuffled towards the free booth.

Thwack! Somebody was getting caned in booth 3.

It wasn't APC Claverhouse's first time in the Ticket Office. Far from it. Last year when she hadn't been keeping up with the payments on her student loans she'd got a six stroke ticket every week she defaulted. She'd been a regular for months until she got the maid job. Being a regular along with her status as a law enforcement officer had brought the privilege of being punished by the sheriff himself.

She saw Sheriff Cockburn coming down the ornate wrought-iron staircase from his Chambers on the second floor. Sheriff Cockburn was young for a sheriff: his father had been a Supreme Court judge and family connections had smoothed his path.

"Hello Justine, long time no see! Let's get booth 2."

She followed him into the booth and handed over her tickets.

"I'm surprised to see you here. I thought you'd got a maid's position to pay off your interest? Oh... it's not the debt this time, environmental and social media misdemeanours... Hmmm... I'd thought you'd be more careful as a police officer..."

"I would be. My mistress sent me to pay her tickets."

The sheriff nodded.

"Well then, I'll let you choose... Strapped hand or caned bottom?"

"I'll take the strapping please."

"OK then. Hold out your hand. You know the drill."

She held out her right hand with the left under it. He was quick and efficient. The tawse came down with a reasonable crack. Not too hard but hard enough.

"One, sir," she nodded and gave him a small smile to indicate she was happy with the intensity of the stroke. After a few months of weekly punishments, the two of them trusted each other.

"Other hand…"

Whack! Both hands stinging now.

"Two, sir!"

Whack! Whack!

"Four, sir!"

Now it was really hurting.

Whack! Whack!

"Six, sir!"

And it was over.

"Thank you, sir." She'd learned to count the strokes and say thank you in the university's 'Receiving Corporal Punishment' module when she was training for the chambermaid job.

"It's been a pleasure, Justine!"

"I'm so glad you were here, sir! I thought I was going to be stuck with one of those bankers, they are vicious."

"I'm always available for you Justine… and tell your mistress that if she gets another ticket and chooses to make payment herself I'd be happy to deal with her personally in my chambers. I'll give you a card for her…"

The sheriff marked her ticket as paid and handed it back to her along with one of his business cards. He could have sent the details to her phone but New Georgians loved quaint old fashioned objects like books and business cards.

She liked the sheriff, he was handsome and always fair with her. She made to shake hands before she left but remembered immediately that her hands had just been strapped and leant forward to give him a kiss on the cheek instead. She felt that they were friends, but kissing on the lips would have been inappropriate because of his social position. Their eyes met for a second as her lips approached his cheek and she saw something stronger than friendship in his eyes. He turned towards her and their lips met. They held the kiss for a second or two. She wanted him to hold her close but she was frozen, unable to take the initiative: both of them feeling the inappropriateness of the situation but neither of them wanted to break off the kiss. Finally, they moved apart, feeling awkward but elated that they had finally kissed.

She walked back up to Ramsay Gardens, her hands still twinging. She'd need to wait a little longer before her MedChip would be allowed to deal with it. She felt relaxed and at peace with the world, a session with the sheriff always relieved tension and she was wondering if maybe there was something more developing between them.

She walked up the spiral staircase to the apartment and found her master and mistress waiting for her. There were excitement and anticipation in the air.

"Did you pay the ticket, Justine?"

"Yes, Madam, and the one from before… they said there was another one already on your file… Here is the receipt."

Dr Streatham looked a little embarrassed.

"Ah...yes, sorry about that. Anyway, I hope it wasn't too sore for you… Your hands look very red!"

"I'm fine, madam. I'm used to the strapping from when I fell behind on my student loan… Oh, the sheriff gave me his card for you…" she fished it out of her pocket and handed it over "… he says if you ever get a ticket again and wish to pay it yourself he would be happy to deal with you in his chambers."

Dr Streatham held the business card gingerly between her fingertips. Not quite sure what to think about this offer.

"You should hold onto that, madam, just in case. Sheriff Cockburn doesn't let people off but, unlike some of the people who buy the right to carry out corporal punishments in the booths, he won't use the strap harder than is necessary."

Dr Streatham put the card away in her purse. Just in case.

That night Justine was invited to her master and mistress's bed even though it wasn't Friday. The next day she was rewarded with a weekend day off and ten euros spending money. She felt really fortunate to have such generous employers.

— ♦ —

Friday, October 7, 2039.

The professor waited in the clean room for the slaughtermen to do their work. As soon as Ms Campbell's head was delivered she locked the outer door, stripped off her clothes and showered, taking extra care when cleaning her face with anti-bacterial soap. Then she sat on the bench which divided the dirty and clean sides of the vestibule to pull on a patient's gown and Tyvek overshoes before rocking over to the clean side. In the second room, the robot surgeons were ready. She put the head in the preparation machine and set the program to harvest the eyes, face and scalp for a transplant.

She lay down on the operating table and rested while the preparation machine carried out its work. Suddenly she heard someone knocking insistently on the clean room door. Annoyed, she went to see what the commotion was about. Out of the corner of her eye, she could see the machine in the next room start the first incisions on the girl's head. Carefully slicing through the layers of skin around her neck then peeling off her face and scalp, putting them on one side like a mask. The next step would be cutting out her eyes, washing them off and placing them on separate stainless steel dishes marked L and R. If they got those switched the professor would be cross-eyed for life. The machines continued removing the girl's skull, preparing the brain for cryogenic storage. She had to die because the professor needed her face but she didn't necessarily need to stay dead forever. The professor told herself it was prudent to keep Victoria's brain frozen just in case it became necessary to find out details of her previous life that only she could know. She wanted to believe she was acting completely logically, like the old professor would have done, but deep down, she knew she could only live with her actions if Victoria was eventually restored to life.

The professor pulled on a clean-room hood and mask before telling the computer to unlock the outer door. The manager was outside holding what looked like a bracelet.

"I'm sorry, madam. We should have noticed this earlier. The girl was wearing a sex-worker bracelet from the brothel. The slaughtermen found it while they were butchering her. If you take her identity you will need to wear it."

That was going to be a problem. The bracelets were designed not to come off until the sentence was served. Pulling one off a corpse was easy enough after its hands were chopped off but getting it onto her own wrist would be far more difficult. Cutting it was not an option: damaging the bracelet or removing it was a crime which would result in an investigation and extra hours being added to the wearer's sentence. She tried to squeeze the bracelet over her hand - it went over her fingers but there was no way it was getting past her thumb and the wide part of her hand. There was only one option in the time available and it wasn't pleasant: she would need to program the surgical robot to dislocate her thumb to allow the bracelet to get past.

Once it had got the bracelet onto her wrist the robot would need to fix the thumb. After she finished with the programming she collected the prepared body parts from the preparation machines, cleaned the bracelet and put it on a metal dish next to Ms Campbell's eyes.

Then it was time. She lay down on the operating table, instructed the computer to begin, and waited for the surgical robot arms to strap her down and put in the IV with the anaesthetic. When she awoke they had finished. Her face, head and left hand were covered in bandages. The anaesthetic was still doing its job and there was no pain - yet. The clone's face was now shredded and flushed down the drain. The link to her previous identity was broken. Neither the farmer or the manager had enough information to link this face to the professor. The farmer had seen the clone's face but not this one. The manager had seen this one and the clone but had no reason to connect the two patients. All she knew was she had a customer with Guilders to spend on a face transplant.

She knew she should have at least a day of rest to recover from the surgery. Even though the robots and the Guild drugs and wound closing technologies were decades ahead of anything generally available, and what was generally available in 2039 was pretty good, it was still a serious procedure. But she didn't have time for that. She got up off the operating table and walked, slightly unsteadily out of the surgical suite, The dead girl's effects were waiting on the dirty side of the entrance room. She took off her surgical gown and threw it in the laundry. Put on the dead girl's clothes. She'd slept for three hours after the surgery. It was now five pm, any longer would be a problem. Hopefully, there had been enough time for the Guild healing gels to regenerate sufficient skin over the wounds. She took off the bandages. Her new face was swollen, the lines where it had been bonded to her head still noticeable at close range but they shouldn't be visible to a CCTV camera on a lamppost fifty metres away in the dark. There was a little pain now as the anaesthetic wore off but she'd have to live with that.

While she had been asleep the manager had used a program provided by the Guild to access the servers of the MedChip company and change Victoria's record so that readings for her account would be taken from the MedChip inside the professor's body rather than the one which was about to be cremated along with Victoria's bones.

Ten minutes later she walked through the front entrance to the slaughterhouse accompanied by the manager. Her face was lowered and she was pretending to sob. Actual sobbing wasn't possible with her newly transplanted eyes. The manager pretended to console her for the benefit of the CCTV. The slaughterhouse records would show that Victoria Campbell had been denied assisted suicide by the management because she'd been drinking and there was concern about her mental health. The manager had let her sleep off the alcohol and then driven her back to her student accommodation. The CCTV at the student halls would show her arriving. No question that the manager was a responsible citizen and Ms Campbell had left the slaughterhouse safe and well. Except that prime cuts of Ms Campbell were now neatly wrapped in greaseproof paper and awaiting delivery to Alexander Bean and Sons delicatessen in Victoria Street.

The professor went through Ms Campbell's possessions. A university matriculation card on a lanyard: plastic ID cards were purely ornamental these days when everything was accessed by a iris scan. The real reason for the card was on the back: her room number and hall were written on it in big letters with a sharpie. Having their address on a card hanging around their neck was a precaution by the university against freshers getting too drunk to remember where they stayed. Her phone. A little bit of money. Hopefully, she had left the rest of her stuff in her dorm room. A laptop would be nice, and some more clothes. And hopefully, she didn't have a roommate who would notice her voice had changed. There were variables that couldn't completely be controlled for in this plan.

They arrived at the Pollok Halls campus and she got out. Her face was really hurting now. She opened the pack of painkillers in her pocket and took one. She'd hoped her MedChip would have been able to regulate the pain on its own so she could keep a clear head but something stronger was needed. She found the right block and looked at the camera next to the door. The iris scan worked and the door clicked open. She followed the signs to her room and passed a few people in the corridor. Nobody noticed anything wrong. Getting off your face wasn't uncommon for a fresher on the first week of term although, usually, it was to do with drink rather than surgery. She looked directly at the sensor on her door so it could scan her iris. The door opened and, thankfully, it was a single room. Victoria's stuff was strewn over the bed and lying in a pile on the floor.

The professor cleared the bed with a sweep of her good arm. She pulled back the sheets, kicked off her shoes, shrugged out of her coat and lay down. Too tired to even think of undoing buttons or zips with her bandaged hand she went to sleep still wearing the rest of her clothes.

She woke up at around midday the next day. Her thumb and face were throbbing like nothing good. She hunted through the small student room for food and discovered a couple of bags of Fuel in the cupboard. Fuel was provided to everyone by the NHS, its composition was customised based on data from your MedChip, your DNA and your patient records to provide exactly the nutrients and medicines you required. The rich would get most of their nutrients from normal meals so their Fuel portions would be small and contain mainly medicines and supplements. If you were poor the Fuel portions would be much larger and provide nutrition as well as medication. The problem with getting nutrition this way was the taste. In the professor's experience, nothing but Brown Sauce could make Fuel taste appetising. She was pretty sure Victoria could not afford Brown Sauce. Nevertheless, she had to eat and drink so she made up Victoria's morning portion of Fuel and sipped away at her unpalatable breakfast until it was done.

Afterwards, she took some painkillers - the pain was still beyond what her MedChip could handle on its own - and started taking inventory of Victoria's clothing, folding it neatly and putting it away in the wardrobe. She had to be at a memorial service tomorrow morning: if Victoria didn't own something appropriate she'd need to go shopping this afternoon. Fortunately, Victoria had a conservatively cut black dress and a dark coloured coat and she had one pair of tights remaining with no ladders. It wasn't perfect but it would do: the deceased wouldn't mind what she wore as long as she showed up.

— ♦ —

Sunday, October 9, 2039.

It was Sunday and the great and the good of New Georgian society were on their way to church. Church attendance had fallen off among the population at large but among the lawyers, landowners and bankers it was almost universal. Justine was expected to attend with her master and mistress. They all dressed formally for church, which in New Georgian society meant in more old-fashioned clothes than normal. Where, on a working day they would merely avoid artificial fibres, zips and such like innovations on Sundays they went for the full 18th-century look. Her Sunday best maid uniform had a long black dress with a low neckline and a white cap. Her mistress too was wearing a Georgian style dress and her master a fetching knee-length coat and breeches. She walked one pace behind them down the Royal Mile towards St Giles. A respectable family, everyone in their place.

This Sunday the eleven am service was also a memorial for Professor Hume, formerly Chief Economic Adviser to the Scottish Government and there were more people attending than usual. The first few pews had been reserved and her master and mistress ended up sitting several rows back, despite arriving early. As a maidservant, she sat at the back of the church, out of sight and not taking one of the good seats from the gentry. The rows at the front were filling up with the professor's friends and colleagues. She recognised the sheriff, arriving with his husband and a teenage daughter. And the chief constable was sitting with his first wife and her boss, Detective Inspector Chisolm. She'd often wondered about whether the chief constable and her boss were in a relationship. They sometimes went for lunch together and on those days the detective inspector occasionally wore a skirt or dress instead of trousers. Nothing wrong with that, it was 2039 and he had as much right to wear a dress as she had to wear trousers. But if the detective inspector was attending a public event like this along with the chief constable and his first wife they must be married. She wasn't surprised: everyone said the chief constable was thinking about moving on to a career in politics and it was politically astute to take a male wife. There were many gay and transgender voters these days, people were more open minded now that even straight couples could no longer afford to have children. Even the New Georgians approved of gay and transgender equality.

The row she was in started to fill up with the servants of the rich and powerful. Only one person looked out of place in the New Georgian ambience of the congregation. A girl of about twenty sitting on her own and wearing modern clothing. She looked exhausted, her face was swollen and one hand was bandaged. Unusual, but it was fresher's week and she wouldn't be the first student to have a little too much to drink and fall over. Her black dress was modest and appropriate for a memorial service but definitely not in the New Georgian style. Maybe she was a science student from the university - but science students would normally scoff at church services and religion. Maybe she knew the professor. She was a bit young to be a postgraduate student... perhaps his mistress or a former maid or a hidden illegitimate child. She smiled, realising she was thinking like a cop, as if the girl was a suspect, when there was absolutely no indication that a crime had been committed.

The organist began to play and everyone stood up to sing the first hymn. She didn't pay much attention to the service. She didn't believe in God and guessed that most of those attending the service didn't believe either. They found it entertaining to suspend disbelief for an hour like you would in the theatre and a useful opportunity for social networking. The eulogies by the professor's colleagues were more interesting. She hadn't realised how influential his economic simulations had been on the political course of the country over the last two decades. The girl in the black dress was paying rapt attention, she wasn't crying and she didn't even seem to be particularly sad. If she had to guess she'd say the emotion on her face was pride. It was curious.

At the end of the service, the minister made a short announcement. The professor and his wife had put money aside in their will to pay for a reception after the memorial service. The reception was being held in the Signet Library across from the church and the whole congregation was invited to attend, whether or not they had known the professor.

Justine's master and mistress were curious to see the Signet Library. It was a historic part of the law courts complex and usually only open to members of the Faculty of Advocates. Renting it for a reception would have been expensive. So they walked over the cobbled square to the reception along with the vast majority of the congregation. The professor's estate had laid on wine and a buffet lunch. Small groups of the gentry were reminiscing about when they had met the professor and his life's work. The girl in the black dress had come too. Standing in the corner by herself sipping a glass of red wine. As a cop, Justine would have liked to go and talk to her but she was here as a chambermaid and she had to stay close to her master and mistress in case they needed her.

The sheriff saw her and came over with his husband to introduce himself to her master and mistress.

"Sheriff Cockburn, pleased to make your acquaintance. I had the pleasure of meeting your maid in an official capacity a few days ago. Did you know the professor?"

"No, we never met him. We've not been in Edinburgh long, we are academics from the US visiting the university. Scottish literature

- here to study the poems of Burns."

"Ahh, the bard." The sheriff began to recite, "When chapman billies leave the street, And drouthy neibors, neibors, meet…"

Dr Streatham continued, "As market days are wearing late, And folk begin to tak the gate…"

The sheriff's husband smiled at her. "I'm afraid I never learned much poetry at school. I'm more of a scientist. I'm Jeffrey, by the way: Jeffrey Frances Cockburn."

"Justine Claverhouse, I'm an apprentice in the police. I have the maid job to help with my student debt."

"Of course… my husband mentioned you to me… He always looked forward to your weekly visits…"

She smiled.

"I did too, to be honest. The sheriff was always fair with me. Not like some of the others. I was very lucky to be able to see him. I didn't realise he was gay…"

"Ohh, he's not. We were first and second husbands of a very special woman. Unfortunately, our wife died a few years ago and it's just the two of us now along with our daughter."

"I'm sorry for your loss. It must be difficult for you."

"Yes, it was some time ago but we still miss her. My husband always tells me when he's dealt with one of your… legal problems… and I'm glad we met so I can put a face to the name."

Justine wasn't sure what to say, she felt her face flush red.

"Oh, don't worry. I'm not jealous… except that I wish I had the same opportunities as Jeffrey." He grinned. "Maybe I should buy some corporal punishment rights and fill in for my husband the next time you have a ticket." He paused, "Seriously, Jeff really likes you and I'd like to get to know you better myself. It wouldn't be appropriate for Jeff to ask but maybe you would like to have dinner with us one evening? When you aren't on duty as a maid and Jeff isn't on duty as the sheriff."

"That would be nice, I'd really love to, but I don't get time off in the evenings. As soon as I'm off duty with the police I need to go straight home and order take-out for my master and mistress. Then I have to fetch it, they don't allow delivery drones in the historic area."

The other three seemed to have changed the topic of their conversation away from Burns. Justine's mistress was asking about the punishment booths. They didn't have anything like that in the US and she was curious to see them.

"Well that's easily arranged." said the sheriff "all you need to do is break a couple of laws….." he laughed, then added

"….but, seriously. It's Sunday and nobody is at work. If you like we can walk over to the courthouse and I'll show you around."

That was a far more interesting offer than staying at the professor's memorial buffet. Their teenage daughter wasn't interested in coming to the courthouse and said she'd walk back home So the five of them went across to the court building. As they crossed the cobbled square in front of St Giles someone swore loudly a few steps behind them. Justine turned to see what had happened: the girl in the black dress from the reception was looking at her hand with a mixture of disgust and disbelief. The top of her head and the shoulders of her dress were splattered with something.

"Fucking pigeons!"

As a maid, Justine always had a small packet of tissues on her person in case she needed to wipe something up so she offered a few to the unfortunate girl. The girl tried her best to get clean but the poo was particularly offensive. It had to be a larger bird than a pigeon and one that had been eating something pretty rank. She thanked Justine and went on her way no doubt eager to get home and have a shower and put her clothes in the washing machine as quickly as possible.

The sheriff waved to the guard and they were buzzed in. He showed them the courtroom that was used for the historic crimes trials, his chambers on the top floor with views over the city and the cells in the basement. Then he took them into the deserted Ticket Office and showed them the separate male and female punishment booths. He opened the door to booth two. The walls were of dark stained wood with decorative carvings. In the middle of the booth was a polished wooden table and hanging on the wall next to it the instruments of punishment. The cane and the strap. A set of leather cuffs hung next to the cane in case the miscreant needed to be restrained. The implements in the female booths were different from those in the male ones. The strap a lighter grade of leather, the cane thinner and not quite as long.

Her mistress had picked up the strap and was examining the workmanship. Leather was an increasingly rare commodity now that cows were no longer farmed for meat. She held the strap close to her face to smell it and feel the texture against the soft skin of her cheek. They all knew what would come next. The inevitable curiosity when you hold an instrument like that. What would it feel like? Her master had picked up the cane, feeling the cool wood run through his hands. His eyes told the same story as his wife's. Curiosity. Unlike actual criminals their MedChips's pain control was still active so they had little to worry about.

The sheriff's husband touched her arm. "I think we should give them a little privacy. Don't you?"

Justine caught her mistress's eye. Her mistress nodded towards the door. A clear instruction.

Justine left with the sheriff's husband. It was obvious what the other three were about to get up to.

"Booth one is free," he said.

Who was she to disagree? Just as they closed the door behind them, they heard the first crack of the strap. Justine wondered which of them was getting it - her master or her mistress.

Justine stood in front of the sheriff's husband wondering what his first move would be. After the kiss at the end of their last encounter, she thought something serious was developing between herself and the sheriff. If she married the sheriff, she'd also be marrying his husband: she'd be wife to both of them. So when the sheriff's husband kissed her she kissed him back. Then they did it again. He was younger than the sheriff and his skin was smoother but he kissed well.

There was a loud crack from the booth next door. Somebody had just been caned. "OUCH!" That was her mistress' voice. Then the sheriff's voice - instructing her master on how to deliver the next stroke properly.

They chuckled as the caning lesson continued. They'd both had plenty of experience with the sheriff.

Justine took out her phone and asked him if she could add him as a friend so they could stay in touch. He nodded. She pointed the camera at his face. The facial recognition found his details immediately. He smiled as she scrolled through the possible categories for the new contact: Customer, Master, Boss… She paused over

'Boyfriend' and he reached over and tapped it for her. He told her to invite the sheriff too. A minute later his phone beeped and asked if he wanted to add her as a 'Girlfriend'. He pressed yes. In the next booth the 'ting' of a message arriving interspersed with the whack of what sounded like the strap. The lesson was moving on. Her phone told her the sheriff had added her as a girlfriend too. It was official: she was dating the sheriff and his husband.

From that point on the three of them messaged each other every day. And Justine had a whole day off the next weekend which she could spend with them.

— ♦ —

Sunday, October 9, 2039.

Life was remarkably pleasant for Archibald Campbell despite being sentenced to death. Sure, there was a policeman posted at the bottom of the spiral staircase which led to his bedroom but that didn't really bother him because he hadn't left his attic bedroom for ten years. There were much grander bedrooms in the palace but he had chosen this one for good reason. For one thing, this minor room could be fitted out with modern furniture and a proper air conditioning system without Historic Scotland noticing, for another when you are as fat as the landlord there is far too much walking involved in getting from one side of a large room to the other. But most importantly this attic bedroom was immediately underneath a small tower topped with a cupola. The tower was the perfect roost for his pigeon.

Ever since he'd bought Holyrood Palace from the royals the spiral staircase up to his bedroom had been a struggle. He told himself that people had been a lot smaller when the palace had been built, which was true. It was equally true that people were still a lot smaller than the landlord. When he first moved into Holyrood Palace he was only twenty-five stone and with a bit of effort, he could squeeze himself between the stone walls on either side of the spiral staircase. After a few years, he had to get the servants to coat the walls with Vaseline to aid his passage. And then, one morning, after a particularly large breakfast in bed he found he simply couldn't fit. Getting down that stone staircase was always more difficult than getting up for some geometric reason that he'd never quite figured out.

There was no way he would be allowed to widen the staircase: Holyrood Palace was under the strictest level of historic building protection. So, the landlord was stuck like Winnie the Pooh until he lost enough weight to fit again. But he really didn't want to stop eating and, when he thought about it, going up and down stairs was a bit too much effort anyway when he had his TV and the controls for his pigeon in the bedroom. Ten years of lying in bed and stuffing his face later he was now thirty-five stone. Walking over to his toilet had been too much effort for the last couple of years so he wore a nappy. There was not the remotest chance of him fitting down that staircase now, and that had turned out to be remarkably convenient when the police had come to arrest him. The police had called Historic Scotland to see if there was any way an exception could be made to the building regulations, to let them knock out a window to extract him with a crane or cut a hole in the floor but had got nowhere. Not a stone or plank of Holyrood Palace could be damaged. In the end, they'd posted a guard at the bottom of the stair and left him to his TV and his pigeon.

The pigeon was the landlord's pride and joy. When he was a child, he'd visited the Camera Obscura and marvelled at the ability it gave to spy on the people of Edinburgh without leaving your house. As an adult, he'd bought the building, but it wasn't really grand enough for someone of his importance to live in. He'd thought about getting a camera obscura fitted to Holyrood Palace, but building control would never allow it and in any case, the palace was at the bottom of the Royal Mile and a camera obscura was only useful if it overlooked the town. So, a few years ago he'd purchased a state-of-the-art drone. Not a boring quadcopter but a robotic bird controlled by your brain via a headset which fitted over your skull. This wasn't fancy Guild technology, the Guild wanted nothing to do with the landlord, just common or garden 2035 vintage electronics and robotics. Once you had the interface trained you could make the bird execute simple flight manoeuvres just by thinking 'UP', 'DOWN' and so on really hard. Primitive but fairly effective. The robotic bird had been designed to look almost exactly like a pigeon. Close up you could see the difference and in flight, it was far less agile but unless you were paying close attention you probably wouldn't notice. When the pigeon was flying high the 360-degree view from its panoramic camera could be projected on the walls and ceiling of the landlord's bedroom, just like the original camera obscura. When he landed the pigeon or wanted to zoom in on something with the pigeon's second camera he could use a second monster screen beside the one that showed daytime TV. The landlord spent hours flying his pigeon over the city and spying on the tenants of his many properties. Looking for any infringement of their rental agreements he might be able to fine them for. Did they have their boyfriend staying with them without disclosing the extra tenant? Or were they drying clothes from the balcony or smoking inside the flat or keeping a pet. The pigeon saw everything. And it had one other function: the servants would syphon up shit from his nappy into a syringe which clipped into a miniature bomb bay in the pigeon's abdomen. The landlord could then command the pigeon to defecate on his many enemies just by focussing on the word 'SHIT'. With the pigeon, daytime TV, and Kentucky Fried Fingers he didn't miss the time when he was light enough to take a trip up the Royal Mile in his sedan chair carried by eight muscular footmen.

Today he had landed the pigeon on top of St Giles. He wanted to watch the great and the good of Edinburgh attending the memorial service for Professor Hume. The professor had never made an attempt to make the landlord's acquaintance and that rankled a little. The landlord was undoubtedly one of the most powerful men in Edinburgh, descended from one of the oldest landowning families in Scotland and yet he was completely cold-shouldered by a mere academic with no property or land to speak of. And there, coming out of the Signet Library was the damn sheriff who had sentenced him to death and put a policeman at the bottom of his stairs. The opportunity was too good to waste. The senior footman in charge of changing his nappy had reported that the contents were especially noxious today as he loaded the syringe into the pigeon. The landlord willed the pigeon to take off and circle over the little group then thought, "SHIT". In his eagerness to release while the target was still in the danger zone he thought so hard about shitting that he filled his nappy again. Above St Giles, the motor in the belly of the pigeon whirred and pushed down the plunger of the syringe expelling the ordure directly above the sheriff and his party.

However, aiming a dose of watery shit from a moving pigeon, outdoors with a breeze blowing is a tricky business and the landlord had little or no coordination. So, not surprisingly, he missed. He didn't mind too much because it splatted onto a girl that had been walking a few paces behind his target. It was almost as much fun to watch her feel her hair to find out what had hit her and see the expression on her face as she discovered her hand was covered in faeces as it would have been to hit his intended target. He enjoyed watching her discomfiture so much he decided to fly the pigeon overhead and follow her all the way home. Maybe he could find somewhere to perch where he could watch her trying to clean up. Quite likely she was one of his tenants and if she was breaking any rules, or even if she wasn't, it would be amusing to follow up his prank with the pigeon with a penalty charge or rent increase.

— ♦ —

The professor had enjoyed hearing the eulogies from her friends and colleagues. Admittedly, there had been a small risk in attending the service. Her new persona of Victoria Campbell had stood out among the mourners and congregation: too young and her clothes too modern. But she'd stayed far enough back at the church that nobody important had noticed and at the reception, everybody just assumed she was a student freeloading for food. Making the reception open to the whole congregation had been a masterstroke.

Then that damned pigeon had wasted her special day. This young female body had a far more acute sense of smell than the old male one, which didn't help at all in a situation like this. It was disgusting. As soon as she got back to her room, she ripped her clothes off and went straight into the shower to get her hair clean. Ten minutes later she emerged smelling much better to face the chore of cleaning up her clothes. She'd stuffed the tissue she'd been given to wipe herself in her pocket because there weren't any bins nearby and the fines for dropping litter were severe. As she picked it up gingerly between finger and thumb to flush it down the toilet - no way she was leaving it in the bin to stink out the room - she felt nauseated. But then her brain started to process what her nose was telling it. That smell wasn't normal for bird droppings. She forced herself to look, the colour was wrong for bird shit too. No white splatter - it was brown, wet and soppy.

Something moved in the corner of her eye. There was a pigeon perched on her window ledge. Looking straight at her. She hadn't bothered to draw the curtains, even though she had just come out of the shower. There wasn't any need, she was on the third floor and nobody could see this far into her room anyway. The bird turned to fly away, and its movement looked somehow unnatural. She didn't think it was a real bird. It could be some kind of winged robot drone. Possibly a peeping Tom had been using it to look into her room. A robot bird would also explain why the excrement did not appear to be of avian origin. It was all too much of a coincidence.

The professor was furious. She might need expert help to find the guilty party and the services of a forensic ornithologist did not go cheap. But if the material was of human origin a simple DNA test followed by hacking into the police database would identify the culprit, she'd try that first. She sealed the shit-stained tissue in a ziplock bag, preserving the evidence.

Which led to a second unpleasant thought. It was possible that her precautions had failed and the perpetrator was somebody who had a grudge against the old professor. If someone had managed to link her new identity to the professor she could afford to take no chances. That damned cop had been at the service. Now he was married to the chief constable he was more of a threat: his new husband might listen to his theories. It was time to tie off the loose end. She could put out a smart contract and pay a small fraction of a Guilder to have him killed with one of the Guild's untraceable bio-weapons but it would be cheaper and more discreet to do it herself.

The Guild had long ago arranged a shadow WiFi network covering the city. There was a backdoor in the internet router provided by the most successful ISP, with the right information you could log in to any of those routers: your traffic would then be routed wirelessly across several hops and emerge looking like it came from a random customer several kilometres away. That gave her an untraceable internet connection and the first thing she was going to do with it was to access the cloud service where the MedChip data were stored.

The MedChips were supplied by a Guild affiliated company and a trivial amount of Guilders bought her access. She tweaked a few of the measurements from Detective Inspector Chisolm's chip: just enough so the software would report a warning and suggest he went to the hospital for tests.

Victoria kept her phone in a faux-leather case, On the inside of the flip-over cover, there was a slot where she'd put a slip of folded over paper. The professor pulled it out and opened it. It was a note scrawled on a greasy sheet of paper which looked and smelled like it had been torn off the corner of the wrapping around a portion of chips:

"Fuck off. If you come back I will sue your mother for a million euros for breaching her non-disclosure agreement. Dad."

Clearly there was tension within Victoria's family and, as the professor went through the e-mails on Victoria's laptop and the texts on her phone, he discovered Victoria also had other troubles: she'd run out of money. The university had billed her for a thousand euros worth of 'extras' beyond the specified course fees covered by her student loan and the landlord of the student accommodation had demanded an extra five hundred euro deposit beyond what was stated in her contract. This was preposterous: Victoria should have got her lawyer on the case and it would have been sorted out by the end of the week. Then she remembered that Victoria had no money and the lawyer the old professor had used billed three hundred euros an hour. She had a look at the bill, Victoria's landlord was Argyll Lettings, Archibald Campbell's company - the owner of most of the student flats in Edinburgh. No surprise that he was ripping off a new tenant. There was only one entry on Victoria's to-do list: 'Watch Archibald Campbell hang.'

The next thing was to check the Scottish Prostitution Service app on her phone to see what Victoria's sentence was and more importantly how many bookings she had outstanding. Now that he had stolen her identity Victoria's problems were the professor's problems. It turned out Victoria hadn't been sentenced. She had signed on with the brothel voluntarily to pay her bills because she was scared of taking on more debt. She'd been putting in a lot of hours but it hadn't been enough to catch up and she was now getting final demands and threats of being barred from her course and evicted from her room. These days MedChips protected you from pain, disease and pregnancy, the omnipresent CCTV protected you from violent crime, education protected you from religious superstition, but nothing protected you from landlords, bankers and compound interest. Faced with the choice of borrowing more money or giving up on university and going back home to the 'Royal McNab' in Pitlochry she'd taken another way out.

To be fair, the drugs the manager of the Escape Room had put in Victoria's tea hadn't helped her state of mind either, but the professor didn't think about that: she was starting to identify with Victoria and her anger was directed against the landlord.

Thankfully, all the bookings after Victoria's appointment at the Escape Room had been cancelled but there were many messages from customers trying to book her again. Idly, the professor started to flip through the messages from Victoria's clients. Most of them were senior citizens. She'd been working two nights a week at an old-folks home and making house calls to several more. The professor smiled when he saw the name of one of her old colleagues, now retired. She wasn't surprised that so many of the customers were pensioners. A few years before a group campaigning for men's rights had taken a case all the way to the European Court of Human Rights. In a landmark ruling the court had decided by seven votes to six (coincidentally there were seven male and six female judges on the panel) that men had a medical need for regular intercourse and it should be recognised as a human right. To comply with the ruling the NHS had started to issue prescriptions for sex once a week to any male who otherwise wouldn't get any, and that included a lot of retired people.

The professor had simulated all this in his work at the Adam Smith Institute for Computational Economics: but now his new persona was experiencing the consequences personally it felt very different. The problem was simple enough to understand without the complex simulations. Most people's labour was no longer worth anything in monetary terms. Either machines could do their job or their work, once done, could be copied. When something could be copied easily competition forced the price down until sooner or later someone started to give it away. As a result, it was near impossible to get paid for software, books, music or any content that could be digitised and downloaded. People don't pay for things they can get for nothing no matter how useful they are. But you can't get housing for nothing: it is a scarce but essential resource and the debt-based economic system rewarded hoarding scarce resources. House prices and rents kept increasing while the price of useful products and services kept falling because prices were almost always determined by scarcity rather than value. Landlords kept getting richer and they used the money they collected in rent to buy more property or lent it out at interest. In a vicious circle, rent and interest were sucking up so much of people's income there was little left to spend on anything else, which depressed every other sector of the economy and made it even harder to earn a living.

Everybody who didn't own property got poorer and more dependent on debt. How do people pay interest on their debt when physical labour and mental labour is worth next to nothing? If they are allowed to walk away from their debt in a system where money is created from debt banks will fail, savings will be wiped out and the value of houses will crash. That isn't acceptable to a government run by people who own houses and have savings in banks. When it saw the simulations of what would happen if debts could not be collected government was clear: if all that debtors had to sell to pay the interest on their debt was their bodies that was what had to happen. The consequence was punishment booths, domestic service contracts, sex work orders and when there was no other option the farms. Paradoxically, the electorate was all in favour. The more they struggled with their own debts the more strongly they felt that others should be forced to pay up. The more they struggled with their rent the more they wanted to be a landlord themselves some day.

Advanced technologies could and should have meant more leisure and more prosperity for everyone. The work at his institute had shown it wasn't difficult to design an economic system which would allow this - if you started from scratch. What was next to impossible was to design a transition away from the existing system. Money isn't just about what you can buy, it is a means of keeping score. Those who are ahead and those who think they can get ahead won't allow the table to be kicked over to start again with different rules. Short of moving to a different planet the professor didn't see how the problem could be solved.

But she had a more immediate concern than her theoretical musings about fractional reserve banking. She was now looking at the 'Personal Details' screen in the brothel app and she saw why she didn't have any future bookings. It wasn't that Victoria had remembered to cancel them. Her status was 'On Leave' and the reason was 'Pregnancy'. Right at the end of her messages, there was one from the madame of the brothel herself. It was an official apology that she had become pregnant while working for them. Her MedChip must be faulty and she should have it checked as a matter of urgency. The brothel would issue an official letter saying the pregnancy was unintentional and she should not worry about being prosecuted for becoming pregnant without a licence. They were willing to offer an ex-gratia payment of a hundred euros a week until she was fit to return to work provided she signed a disclaimer and promised not to sue.

The professor suddenly felt faint and had to lie down. That message had come in this morning: after Victoria was dead and the health monitoring for her account had been switched to use the professor's own MedChip. Which meant it wasn't Victoria that was pregnant it was the professor.

Brown Sauce and Chips

Monday, October 10, 2039.

When Detective Inspector Chisolm woke up, the first thing he saw was the notification on his phone. His MedChip was recommending he went to the hospital as soon as possible to have a check-up. It wasn't unheard of for there to be a false alarm but MedChips had sensors in direct contact with your blood and were generally accurate. He showed his husband.

"You better take the morning off and go straight away. Don't worry: if there is something the MedChip will have found it in plenty of time. Text me as soon as they tell you anything."

There was no doubt that Bobby was right. He opened the NHS app on his phone and set up an appointment for this morning. The hospital would be sent the data from the MedChip and be ready to do the correct tests. After breakfast, he summoned a car and was driven to the New Royal in Little France. He had to wait for an hour before he was seen but after that, the service was extremely efficient. They had installed the latest diagnostic machines from a company on the biotech campus right next to the hospital. The nurse showed him to the diagnostic suite where the machine performed a scan of his entire body. He went back to the waiting room while the computers ploughed their way through the terabytes of image data looking for anomalies. An hour later he was called to a different room, something had shown up on the scan and they were going to take a biopsy. He had to remove his clothes and lie face down on the table while a robotic arm injected a local anaesthetic and then carefully pushed an extremely fine needle into his scrotum. The biopsy sample taken, the machine applied a sticking plaster and moved to the next location. Two samples from separate potential tumours would be enough. The detective inspector was sent home to await an e-mail from the hospital once the samples had been processed.

The professor had set up programs to notify her as soon as the hospital requested the detective inspector's data and she was ready to set in motion the next step of her plan. The company which leased the diagnostic machines to the hospital was a spin-off business from the university, owned by a Guild affiliated professor of robotics. It was the same company which made the machines that had performed the professor's surgery but the equipment it supplied to the NHS was a lot less advanced. For a small payment in Guilders, the professor could obtain access to the cloud server with the patient images and the company had helpfully provided a program to do exactly what was needed in this case. The shadows of tumours were added to the images, carefully calculated based on analysis of thousands of real tumours to pass scrutiny even by a trained eye. The largest one was in the left testicle. Still too small to feel with a finger, not that doctors bothered with manual examinations these days, but more than large enough for the medical scanner to find.

She waited until the results of the biopsies were uploaded and made another set of careful alterations. The biopsies now showed the detective inspector had cancer, the DNA tests on the tumour said it would not respond to chemotherapy. Along with the imaging showing multiple secondaries the prognosis was not good.

The final step was a small adjustment to the detective inspector's Fuel prescription. Like many people he was getting a small dose of antidepressants, her plan would work faster if that was stopped.

In the old days, the Guild would have used a tick to inject their target with cancer cells genetically engineered from the target's own DNA. Untraceable death by natural causes and all that was necessary was to arrange for a tiny biting arachnid to fall into the victim's hair. These days the professor was subtler, she preferred to get the same effect without physically harming the victim at all. Just a little nudge to persuade them to do what was necessary. Of course, if the nudge didn't work the original approach was still available.

— ♦ —

Wednesday, October 12, 2039.

The surprising thing is just how smoothly and silently society deals with death. The day after his hospital visit the detective inspector got another e-mail: they'd set up an appointment with the consultant. The interview started with "Mr Chisholm I'm afraid it's not good news" and it went downhill from there. The imaging and lab results were conclusive. Cancer and it had already spread. The tumour DNA had been analysed and they were not predicted to respond to chemotherapy. The only available treatment would be radical surgery, followed by intensive radiotherapy, it would be painful and leave him very weak, it might even kill him. Due to the low probability of success, the NHS would not fund it. It could be done privately but the consultant would not recommend it, it might be better to enjoy the last bit of time he had while he was still healthy enough to get about. The cancer was likely to progress rapidly.

The consultant said he was sorry again and got ready to leave. Consultants don't hang about when you are an NHS patient. He left him with a nurse who would be able to explain his options. The nurse was about forty and wore a smart skirt suit rather than a uniform. Her name tag read, "Nurse Specialist. End of Life Care".

Detective Inspector Chisholm was too fazed by the whole situation to take in much of what she was saying. The gist was he should think about his options. She would send some information to his phone. He should read it and phone her up if he had any questions. There would also be an official letter which he would need when he decided what he wanted to do.

He got back home and poured himself a large whisky. After it took effect he started to look at the electronic leaflets she had sent. A couple of NHS ones about being a cancer patient and what to expect from the treatment. A couple from charities about support groups. A couple more from charities asking for donations in his will. Two from hospices. A few from undertakers. These days, like everything else, dying had come to be about shopping. And then there were the euthanasia providers. Three of them. The first was a high-end service in a castle with chauffeur transfers and a week's accommodation offering "A death to remember." Then there was a medical research facility that would pay you for donating your body. And finally, the one that caught his eye, because he'd seen the name before. On the professor's death certificate. The Escape Room. Guaranteed swift and professional. Ecologically sound too, your body would be sold as food and they would make a donation to a charity in your name. Or you could pay for their service and the meat would be supplied ready to cook to whoever you nominated. Personal service in your home was possible for an extra charge. The address was an industrial unit near the bypass. He remembered seeing it when he drove past on the A71, a nondescript steel shed, next to the factory that made Brown Sauce. Brown Sauce, like Irn Bru, was a national institution in Scotland. It was about the only thing that could make the vegetables they were forced to eat these days at all palatable to a Scotsman but it was expensive. The days of getting 'salt and sauce' free with a poke of chips were long gone.

The last item was an official form from the consultant. It stated that he had been diagnosed as terminally ill and was eligible for end of life care. There were a couple of notes underneath. Remains suitable for organ donation: No. and Remains suitable for human consumption: Yes.

If he only had a few weeks to live the detective inspector was going to spend them on something that interested him: the Guild investigation. He took medical leave so he could work on it full time. The walls of the home office in Springvalley Gardens were soon covered in pictures of suspects and diagrams showing the connections between them. He was still keeping everything on paper: using the computer was too much of a risk.

The hospital had set up an appointment for the end of life care nurse to visit him at home. He was so deep into the case notes he'd forgotten about it and was surprised to see her at the door. He let her in and showed her to the lounge, hurriedly shutting the door to the home office as he passed. He offered her coffee and she got down to business.

"How are you doing, any pain yet?"

"I'm still feeling fine. I could be imagining it, but I think the lump may be getting bigger."

"Well, you can still decide to get treatment if you want. They'd remove your testicles and get rid of the lump but the problem is it has already spread. Radiation would help but it would come back. Treatment might extend your life, but you wouldn't have much quality of life…"

Months of pain and lying in a hospital bed starting with cutting his balls off and ending with death didn't sound like a great option.

"So what about my other options. The hospice… Tell me the truth, don't sugar coat it…"

"Yes, there's a bit of a waiting list for the hospice so you want to get your name down quickly. It's very nice, they'll take good care of you. The Scottish end-of-life protocol is called the Castlemilk Care Pathway: it has the same dose of opiates as the Liverpool Care Pathway they use in England but with vodka on the side. Your family can visit whenever they want. The last couple of weeks you'll be too weak to get out of bed, then they'll stop feeding you, and eventually, they'll stop giving you anything to drink. It's medical ethics: they can stop giving you what you need to stay alive and dope you up so you don't know what's happening but they can't actually kill you."

Telling her not to sugar coat it had been a mistake.

"Then there are the less conventional options. Quite a few patients are going that way now, but I'm not supposed to recommend them because they aren't NHS services."

"So why would anyone choose them instead of the hospice?"

"Mostly, people choose them because there's no wasting away, you go while you are still healthy enough to get about on your own and it is over the same day. Doctors aren't allowed to take part in euthanasia so they can't administer pain medicine or sedatives but the methods they use are so fast there's no need. "

Detective Inspector Chisholm went back to his files, trying not to think about his own future. There was one case in particular where it looked like a technically advanced criminal network might have been involved: a report of hacking at an internet service company. Several customers from high technology businesses had complained that their e-mail stored on the cloud service must have been read because secret information appeared to have been leaked. It was investigated and a manager at the cloud hosting company fell under suspicion. There was no direct evidence but it was decided to invite him for questioning. The day before the appointment negotiated with his lawyers he died.

He brought up the database of deaths again and looked up the death certificates for the suspects from previous cases in his file. Many of them had been filed by the same euthanasia company as the professor and his wife. The one on the industrial estate beside the bypass: Alexander Bean and Sons Ltd., trading as The Escape Room. He looked up the address on the crime database to see if there had been any other incidents reported to the police at the location. Just a request from Europol to look into the company next door which was suspected of breaking single market food labelling regulations. The Brown Sauce company.

The detective inspector started to form a plan, a crazy plan, but when you've only got weeks to live crazy isn't a problem. He logged into the police computer and created an active investigation for the EU's request. The obvious person to assign to it was his apprentice, APC Claverhouse. She had just completed her internship. Top of her class at university. She was logging the mandatory experience as an apprentice before applying for a paid position. He sent her an e-mail to initiate surveillance on the Brown Sauce factory and the unit next door. Review the CCTV from all the nearby cameras over the last week, capture pictures of people and number plates. He would see if the surveillance produced any leads: maybe the crazy part of the plan wouldn't be necessary.

— ♦ —

Friday, October 14, 2039.

The next evening the detective inspector read the first report APC Claverhouse had filed on the surveillance. She had found several networked CCTV cameras with views of the front and back of the target buildings. She'd looked at the live feeds and the archived footage from the last few days.

Her summary of the surveillance was simple: every couple of hours a minibus arrived loaded with people. The people went into the building, none of them came out. Every now and then somebody was dropped by a car outside, went into the building, didn't come out again. A few people arrived with family members and the family members left after about half an hour carrying plastic bags. What you would expect from a euthanasia facility. She'd concentrated on getting face-shots of people on the way out, rather than the 'customers', she thought she'd got all of the staff. There was a black van coming and going from time to time. Plates showed it was registered to the euthanasia company.

There was another report about her surveillance of the Brown Sauce factory but the detective inspector wasn't interested in Brown Sauce. Except on his chips. The thought of chips reminded him he hadn't eaten. So he went to the chip shop around the corner to get a fish supper with Brown Sauce. Fish was about the only animal protein you could still eat and it was expensive, as was Brown Sauce, but this wasn't the time for penny-pinching.

The detective inspector copied the pictures of people of interest over to the facial recognition program: maybe somebody had a record. Then he ran the plates on the black van on the number plate recognition camera database. It was showing up regularly on the City Bypass - not surprising, given that the company was located only a couple of blocks away from the bypass also quite often on the A701 and A702. Heading south down towards the borders. That was more interesting. After the shopping malls on the edge of town and the university campus at Bush Estate, there wasn't much on those roads except small towns and farms. There was no record of it crossing the border into England: an electric vehicle wouldn't be much use in England anyway.

All three staff members were identified from facial recognition. A woman, Helen McDougal and two men, William Barker and William Harrison. The woman had been employed as a secretary by the university. Fifteen years ago she'd been fired for dishonesty and as a result, had a file on the police computer: she'd been issued a caution since it was her first offence. These days she'd have been fined: the government was too desperate for revenue for the courts to let anyone off without a fine. She'd been unemployed for a while but when contract law was strengthened and people could sign away their legal status as humans making euthanasia possible she was offered the manager's job at the Escape Room.

Mr Barker had been a servitor at the university, in the same department as Ms McDougal and had been let go at the same time. The two men had worked together on the improvements to the Union Canal and then for an abattoir. They had been made redundant when farming animals for meat was banned and shortly after that Ms McDougal had hired them to work at the Escape Room. During one of their periods of unemployment they'd been questioned about a mugging, the victim had a bleeding nose but was otherwise unhurt. Other offences were suspected, but there wasn't enough evidence to file charges. They were definitely persons of interest but they didn't look like criminal masterminds. More like the muscle for someone else.

Inspector Chisholm poured himself a glass of his husband's best whisky. Whisky, fish, chips and Brown Sauce. Not a bad final meal for a Scotsman. All that was missing was a deep-fried Mars bar. He'd been thinking about what the end-of-life nurse had said. Going quickly before you got too ill rather than slowly wasting away in a hospice. Maybe this wasn't so crazy after all. When Bobby got back from work he would talk it over with him.

Inspector Chisholm didn't want to wait until the symptoms were too painful for his MedChip to block out. The professor's changes to his medication were starting to take effect. All he could think about was cancer eating away inside him and death. Life wasn't worth living and there wasn't any point in delaying the inevitable. He spent the morning collecting together his notes on the Guild. It was important that everything was there and that somebody else would be able to follow his train of thought, he was going to hand them over to his apprentice. He added a warning that she should not use computers for anything related to this case. He'd broken that rule quite a few times himself in the last couple of days. But he didn't have anything to lose.

The Escape Room's brochure said no appointment necessary: all that was needed was a letter from a medical professional confirming you were terminally ill.

— ♦ —

Saturday, October 15, 2039.

Everything was done. A final sip of Dutch courage from the whisky bottle for the detective inspector and the chief constable summoned a car to take them to the Escape Room. Bobby had understood why his husband preferred the quick option to the hospice but he thought he should at least wait until he had some symptoms. When it was clear that Duncan's mind was made up he'd insisted on coming with him for support.

They stopped a little back from the building and took out the signal relay for the bug the detective inspector was going to place in the Escape Room. I\t would be his final act as a police officer. The relay would receive the low range, low power radio signal from the bug and use its own more powerful transmitter to upload any received audio and video to the internet. An unremarkable grey metal box, attached to a lampost with a shiny metal tie a few feet off the ground. Nobody would give it a second look. The batteries would last for about a month.

They walked past the Brown Sauce factory. The ground was sloping and the industrial estate was cut into the side of the slope to make a level space to build on. As a result, the yard at the back of the units and the ground floor of the metal sheds was one story below street level at the front. A concrete ramp from the pavement bridged over a narrow gap and pedestrians entered the unit on the first floor. The heavy hardwood door was painted in black gloss with a shiny metal numeral five in the middle. To one side was a polished brass plate inscribed: "The Escape Room. Press for Attention." Then in small lettering at the bottom of the plate: "Alexander Bean and Sons, Ltd." The door and sign were understated and respectable, out of place in this environment: more like what you would expect on an accountant's office in a Georgian tenement in the New Town than a metal shed on an industrial estate.

The chief constable pressed the brass button immediately under the sign. There was a buzz and the door clicked open. They walked into a small waiting area. Directly in front of them was a counter with a middle-aged woman in a blue uniform skirt and jacket. Her name badge said "Helen". She was the one from the surveillance yesterday. To their left was a door designed to look like the entrance to a jetbridge in an airport. Beside it was an illuminated sign: "Now Boarding". There was a large double-glazed glass window running along that side of the waiting area. It looked into a smaller neighbouring room which was configured like the cabin of a plane. Four rows of four aeroplane seats, two seats on either side of a central aisle and lockers for hand luggage above each seat. At the back of the cabin was a toilet and beside the toilet a small service station with a tray bearing plastic cups of orange juice and water. Visitors in the reception area who had accompanied friends or family members were looking through the glass and waving to their relations in the plane seats.

Above the counter were two monitors labelled 'Departures' and 'Remains Reclaim' and on the opposite side of the room a conveyor belt emerged from a gap in the wall covered with a curtain of rubber strips. It looped around and returned into the back of the building through another covered gap. Behind the desk, a closed door led into the body of the facility.

"Hello Dear, can I help you?"

"..... I was given your leaflet at the hospital...."

"Oh yes. that's fine. No problem at all. Can I see your letter?"

Detective Inspector Chisholm fished out the letter from the hospital and handed it to her. She held the QR code on the bottom under a camera attached to her computer. The details appeared on her screen.

"Fine, fine.... look into the camera please, I just need to ask a couple of questions and get it on the record...."

He looked into the camera.

"Do you wish to use our assisted suicide services?"

"Yes"

"Do you accept that to use our service you must accept the legal status of a farm animal?"

"Yes"

"Will you sell us your remains for five hundred Euros. The money to be donated to charity."

"Yes"

"Which charity would you like to nominate."

"The Police Benevolent Fund."

"Well, that's it. All done. Bend forward for me.... we need to give you a tag before you board. It's just so we know who's who... afterwards.."

He leaned forward.

"It goes in your ear. It'll just sting for a second... Face right...."

He faced right and closed his eyes. Felt something cold on his left ear. Then a click and a short pain as it was pierced.

"All done. That wasn't too bad, was it? You can go through now. We've still got a few empty seats so you have time to get some water and use the toilet."

He hesitated.

"Go on through now. Nothing at all to worry about, and it's too late for second thoughts anyway now you're tagged."

Suddenly he was really scared.

"Board now, the toilet is at the back of the cabin."

Probably everybody had the same reaction.

He went straight through the cabin into the toilet and emptied everything. Bowels, bladder, vomit, everything. Then he pulled himself together. Washed his face. Washed his mouth out. Smoothed his hair back. Looked in the mirror above the sink - there was a white plastic cattle tag with a QR code attached to his left ear. He wasn't sure what to do with the bug in his pocket. It would stick under a desk or chair to record audio and video. He could leave it in the plane cabin or take a chance and take it with him when his turn came. But he might not have a chance to stick it to anything after he left the cabin. The end-of-life nurse from the hospital had said it was very fast.

He composed himself and walked back into the cabin. In front of him were four rows of aeroplane-style chairs, four seats in each row. Above the seats were luggage lockers and a panel with ventilation, lights and so on. Just like on a plane. There was a TV screen at the front of the cabin and plastic cups of water and juice on a tray near the back of the cabin. He grabbed a cup of orange juice and drank. His throat was so dry. Everyone in the cabin had a plastic cattle tag attached to their ear. Different colours: to mark whether their organs were suitable for transplant and if their meat was fit for human consumption. Some of the passengers were looking at the TV screen, but the ones in the front row were staring at the door at the front of the cabin. They figured they would be first.

There were empty seats in the back row. He took the first empty seat. Leaned forward as if he was tying his shoelace and stuck the bug under the seat in front, making sure the camera was facing forward.

The woman from reception came into the plane cabin, closing the door to the reception area behind her. She hit a switch and the lights in the room dimmed and changed to a pleasant orange glow. The TV screen lit up showing a smiling woman in the company uniform, standing in the room they were in.

"Welcome to the Escape Room. Please fasten your seatbelts at this time. Your journey will soon begin. The cabin crew will assist anyone that has difficulties with their belt."

Each seat had a lap belt just like in an aeroplane. The detective inspector pulled it around his waist and clicked it into the buckle. There was a buzz and a click and the belt pulled tight. He tried to loosen it but the buckle seemed to be locked.

The flight attendant checked everyone had their seatbelt on properly.

The smiling woman in the video pointed up toward the ceiling.

"Nooses will descend from the panels above your head...."

Panels opened in the ceiling and a noose dropped in front of each of them.

"Place the noose around your neck like this, adjust like this with the knot behind your right ear. If your neighbour is unwell please put on your own noose before helping them with theirs."

The woman from reception passed through checking everyone had their noose correctly in place.

"And now... bon voyage!"

The video stopped and was replaced by a count down.

10...9...8...7...6...5...4...3... There was a whirr and extra slack was paid out into each noose. 2... His seatbelt clicked open... 1...

There was a loud click and suddenly he was falling through the floor.

Outside in the waiting area, the screen marked "Departures" lit up.

There was a muted whir as a motor drew a beige coloured curtain across the window, hiding the taught ropes and the gaping holes in the floor from the eyes of the waiting relatives.

— ♦ —

The detective inspector was falling, quickly until he passed the level of the floor, then much slower and stopping. Loud snapping noises came from all around.

He wondered what had happened? He definitely wasn't dead. The noose around his neck was still slack. They'd botched it, the rope was too long.

He looked around - and immediately wished he hadn't. On each side of his chair, there were shiny L shaped beams of metal. The panel at the bottom of the chair was designed to slide down between these columns. His chair had stopped in mid air. Just before the noose would have come tight.

The seat next to him had fallen all the way to the floor a few metres below. It's previous occupant was dangling a few feet off the ground. Legs still twitching. Head bent over to one side at a grotesque angle. It looked like the occupants of all the rows in front of him were all hanging in mid air, at slightly different heights according to the drop which had been calculated, necks snapped, some of them still twitching.

He felt like throwing up. Someone was crying. He looked to see where it was coming from. Looking more closely, there were two other seats where the passenger was still in their chair rather than dangling in mid air.

There was a whirring noise and his seat started to move again. Very slowly downwards. The rope around his neck came tight. he was suspended in mid air by the noose. He couldn't breathe.

A door opened and the two male suspects they had identified yesterday came in. They walked around taking pictures of everyone as they hung in mid air. One of them pushed him a little to one side to be sure the photo captured the tag in his ear. Then a whirr as the noose gradually lowered until his feet just touched the ground. He had to stand up straight and couldn't get away but he could breathe again. He gasped for air.

"So, just our first class guests left then," said the slaughterman, "don't worry, we'll get round to you, I hope you enjoyed the ride."

"Computer, lower 4A!" The guy next to the detective inspector was lowered down to the floor. The man in the apron slackened the noose round his neck and removed it. Checked for a pulse. He dragged the corpse off the seat and dumped it unceremoniously on the concrete floor at one side of the row of seats.

They were in the body of the industrial unit, one floor down from the reception area with the mock plane cabin. It was a huge concrete-floored space. A metal guiderail ran along about three metres off the ground all along that side of the industrial unit. Hanging off the guide were wire ropes ending in a pair of leather cuffs. The slaughterman buckled the cuffs around the corpse's ankles then pressed a button and the winch at the top wound it in pulling the corpse up until it was hanging with its head a little off the ground. He worked efficiently, removing its clothes and taking off the jewellery and watch and putting them neatly in a plastic tray. Then he slid the naked corpse, along the guide away from the block of chairs. The guide passed over a long metal trough, he pulled the corpse to the far end of the trough, lowered it slightly so its neck was under the level of the trough, picked up a large knife which was stuck to a magnetic strip on the wall and slit its throat. Blood started to flow into the trough. The heart had long since stopped but gravity did the work.

"Computer: reset 4A!" The motor whirred and the noose retracted back up into the ceiling far above us. Then the chair glided up between the guide posts and clicked into its previous position. Upstairs, in the waiting room, the first name and seat number appeared on the departures screen.

His partner was already pulling the body from 3A along the guide to join the first one draining into the shiny steel trough.

It took them about ten minutes before all the bodies were stripped and draining into the trough. The trough was angled slightly so the blood flowed to the far end and into a white plastic waste pipe. The pipe led to the far end of the unit and passed through the wall. Into the Brown Sauce factory next door.

"Right then! Our first class passengers: 1D, 3C, 4B. Just the three of you today. Let's get you tied up…"

His colleague came over with an armful of restraints. He pulled the detective inspector's shirt up and passed a leather belt round his waist, next to the skin and buckled it shut in front. Leather cuffs buckled round his wrists and clipped to the belt. Once he was safely restrained the slaughterman removed the noose. There were three of them left. The detective inspector, a fat man with a beard and a young woman in her early twenties.

"OK then, 1D. The computer says there's nothing wrong with you."

"You're letting me go?"

"Of course not, your death certificate is already filed along with a picture of you hanging with a noose round your neck. It's just there's more money in selling a healthy young woman like yourself to a dairy farm than turning you into burgers. You'll need to wait until I've finished with the others, then I'll drive you down."

"Right, 3C. It says here you've got inoperable cytomyo… something…"

"Yes. The doctors said they couldn't do anything about it, the surgery would be too complex…"

"Well, the Guild is going to give the surgery a go. You're going to be a test subject for the new software on their robotic surgeon and their fancy new laser scalpel."

"Do you really think it can cure me?" The man's voice cracked with emotion and hope.

"Most likely. Their kit is really good. Your problem is that after the robot gets rid of the cytomyo thing it's going to keep going with the rest of the scalpel tests and those will leave you in a fair number of pieces. Look at it this way, you're no worse off than if we'd hung you and then they'd done their scalpel tests on the corpse but it is far more useful to medical science to do the tests on a live body with the heart still beating."

3C didn't completely agree with this ethical argument, but the slaughterman was not interested in further debate. He was put in a wheelchair and wheeled away towards a partitioned-off room on the right of the facility.

"Which leaves 4B," he looked at the Detective Inspector, then glanced at his iPad again.

"OK, 4B the bad news for you is the Guild have bought your body and put a note on your file not to hang you before processing. They don't want your neck damaged. I'm afraid this is about to get messy."

They frog marched the detective inspector over to the beam. Hooked the wire up to the cuffs around his ankles and pulled him into the air. Slid him along to the end of the line of bodies. Picked up the knife and slit his throat. He felt the warm blood shoot out. The slaughterman jumped back. He could see his blood running down the trough. There was a pain in his chest and he was getting cold, cold and tired. Really tired. He felt a hand on his face and something cold against his neck. Sawing through it. Then nothing.

Upstairs, the final name appeared on the departures screen. The relatives' eyes turned to the remains reclaim monitor.

— ♦ —

William Harrison, the second slaughterman, held the head carefully as his colleague, William Barker, separated it from the spine. As soon as the head was free he carried it away. Then Mr Barker went to the front of the queue of bodies and pulled the first one, which had by now stopped dripping blood, along the rail to the steel processing tables. He told the computer to put on his work playlist and the voice of Louis Armstrong filled the factory floor. He picked up a power saw and began to dismember the body. Chopping off the arms and head, then cutting the torso away from the legs. Placing the various parts on the steel table in front of him. The last task was unbuckling the dangling legs from the ankle cuffs. Then he grabbed the metal rope and pulled it around the loop at the end of the rail and back to the start again, lowering the ankle cuffs back to the ground and leaving it ready for when the next set of customers dropped in. Louis Armstrong was just launching into 'It's a wonderful World' as the slaughterman walked back to start work on the next body.

Meanwhile, his colleague had carried the detective inspector's head over to a lab area partitioned off from the rest of the factory floor. A door with a rubber seal around it opened into a changing area where the clean room suits hung. To transit to the clean area you had to sit on a low partition and swing your feet over, your outdoor clothing and shoes never left the dirty side of the partition. The manager was already on the clean side wearing a Tyvek clean room overall. Hair tucked away under a cap. Clean room booties over her feet. She took the severed head from the slaughterman and he returned to his duties.

In the clean area, next to the machine which had excised the professor's hippocampus a few weeks earlier, was a second chest-high metal box. Like the first, it was bolted to the concrete subfloor to stop any vibration. She opened the casing and placed the severed head on the stage. Placed metal clamps over the jaw on either side and screwed them into the bone. Checked that everything was firm and it was totally locked down. Shut the lid which snapped into place, rubber flanges producing an airtight seal. She pressed the big green button on the front of the machine and took a seat. There was a hum as the high voltage power supply in the base of the machine came to life. A red light came on "Danger X-Ray" as the machine began to CT scan the head, building a detailed digital map. A rack of computer equipment next to the box was already calculating a 3D model of the head and deciding on the sequence of cuts. A few seconds after the CT scan finished it was ready. A second light on the front of the box lit up "Laser On". Light from the powerful industrial laser in the base of the box was transferred through a fibre optic cable to emerge at the tip of a robotic arm. The arm moved up to the top of the head and started to cut away the skull sliver by sliver. A complex choreography of moves gradually shaving away the head to expose the brain within. A second robotic arm with a suction tube moved around clearing away the debris. The arms moved faster than any human surgeon ever could and with absolute precision. Second by second, the skull was eroding away and the brain was being exposed.

A hatch in the back of the unit opened and a robotic handling system moved the brain on to the next processing machine. Almost all the skull was gone, just leaving enough bone for the machines to use to firmly clamp their workpiece. The hatch on the back of the second machine clicked shut. No high power lasers in this unit. Instead, multiple delicate robotic arms tipped with surgical tools and high-resolution cameras to complement the CT scan data. The robots were preparing the nerve endings and the ends of the main veins and arteries in the neck. Picking up complex connectors and attaching them to the biological material using special adhesives. The plumbing to connect the arteries and veins which supplied the brain to a new blood supply and the interface between the brain's optic nerves, auditory nerves and nerves from the spinal column to electronic signals. The robotic arms worked quickly and soon all the connectors were in place, tubes and cables leading to the bottom of the plastic panel onto which the brain had been mounted. An arm moved a plastic dome over the top of the brain and clicked it into place on the base panel. The two were fused together by a small laser. A pump started and the dome slowly filled with a transparent fluid, air bleeding out through a vent at the top. Then a green light came on: the lid of the machine could be opened.

The manager took the packaged brain and put it in a carrying chest. The connectors on the bottom of the plastic housing mated with those on the carrying chest. A transfusion bag of chilled O-negative blood was in the next compartment to the brain and a small pump in the base of the chest. Blood circulation was restored two minutes and nineteen seconds after the detective inspector had been decapitated. She closed the transport case lid and the refrigeration unit within started to lower the temperature. She picked up the chest and took it to the partition between the clean and dirty area where Dr Knox's student was waiting to collect it. Then she set the machines to clean out any contamination before their next customer.

Outside Mr, Harrison was still hard at work filleting the woman from 1A. Her relatives had paid extra for first class so she'd be first in the queue for cremation and they wouldn't need to wait so long. Not that it mattered. Once she finished in the clean room the manager filled one of the plastic urns with two scoops of the ash from the bin next to the cremator. When it came down to it one scoop of ash was the same as another and there was plenty left from yesterday. She wasn't going to waste gas running the oven for the leftover pieces of just one body. Gas was expensive these days because of the taxes on greenhouse emissions. She collected the tray of 1A's clothes, folded them neatly and put them in a carrier bag with the company logo. Then she placed the urn and the bag with the effects back in the tray and put it on the conveyor belt. The next tray to go on the belt was 4B.

Upstairs a yellow light started to flash above the belt. The remains collection screen lit up and 1A's name appeared. Her relatives were already impatient, they collected her ashes and personal effects and hurried off back to their lives. The chief constable stood by the belt, fighting back tears as he waited to collect the personal effects and ashes of his second wife, passenger 4B.

Downstairs, the girl from 1D was also waiting. Sitting on the floor and shaking with fear as she watched the slaughtermen at work. They'd put a collar on her and clipped it to one of the pillars that supported the roof so she couldn't run about. The first slaughterman had now finished dismembering the bodies. He took off his apron and washed his hands at a sink near the processing table. Slipped out of his work overshoes. Grabbed his coat.

"Right then, love. Time to take you to the farm. You'll be there in plenty of time to get something to eat before bed. You'll like the farm. I mean the induction isn't pleasant but once it's over you'll get used to the life, it's peaceful, lots of fresh air and nothing at all to worry about."

The black van was parked at the loading dock at the back of the unit. He opened the rear doors and put the girl in the cage. Slammed it shut. Got in the front of the van and told it to drive to the farm, the location was already entered in its GPS. The van software calculated the best route through the traffic, opened the metal shutter over the loading bay, and set off. The slaughterman played a game on his phone as it drove.

Stuck underneath seat 3B the bug planted by Detective Inspector Chisholm was quietly transmitting video and audio to a server on the internet.

— ♦ —

The chief constable summoned a car and sat in it not sure where to tell it to go. The plastic bag with the detective inspector's effects and the urn with his ashes were on the seat beside him. He didn't know what to do: but he felt he had to do something. He definitely didn't want to go home to the house he'd shared with Duncan. He drove around the corner and parked on a side street with a view into the service yard behind the Escape Room. He may as well do some surveillance while he collected his thoughts. He was starting to feel something wasn't quite right about this place. He'd worked his way up through the ranks to the chief constable job and although he'd been in management for many years he still had the instincts of a detective.

There was a different van parked at the loading dock at the back of the Escape Room. A small red van like the ones used by the university, but it didn't have a university logo. Somebody that hadn't shown up in the surveillance before was looking up at the CCTV camera and being let in. A few minutes later he came out carrying a small plastic chest, like something you'd use to keep food cool on a picnic. Male, in his twenties, overweight, wearing jeans, trainers and a sweatshirt with a picture of the cowboy from the video game. Looked more like a student than an undertaker. On a whim, the chief constable decided to follow the van. It was probably nothing, but he had nothing better to do.

The van set off west, towards the bypass, once on the bypass it looped around the southern edge of town and came off at the A701, heading south. Whoever it was, they were probably going home, most people couldn't afford to stay in the city any more. Past the shopping malls built strategically just outside the city limit so as to avoid the city's taxes. After the malls, it was out into the countryside. Then, at a roundabout that seemed far too large for the roads it connected, the van turned off the main road and into the Bush Estate, a university science campus, whose main claim to fame was the Roslin Institute where Dolly the Sheep had been cloned. The campus was large, parkland and woods, the cluster of university buildings which had overflowed from King's Buildings not yet expanded to fill more than a fraction of the space at Bush. The van drove straight past the modern, glass-fronted, three and four-story buildings and turned onto a smaller single track road, winding through the trees for another kilometre, until it came to a dead end at a two-story brick building, out on its own in the woods with nothing around it. The main campus had signs everywhere but this windowless building was unmarked. With the high voltage cables entering it from a nearby pylon, it looked like a large electricity substation. The driver got out of the van, looked up at the CCTV camera mounted beside a heavy metal door and waved. The door buzzed open as he approached and he went in carrying his plastic case.

There were CCTV cameras discreetly placed all around the building and if the chief constable got any closer he'd be seen for sure. Which could be embarrassing because he wasn't certain what was happening was any of his business. A trip from a euthanasia facility to an unmarked university building was certainly unusual but maybe it was all legitimate. Someone might have given permission for their body to be used for science. Or maybe it was a defence project and nothing good would come of sticking his nose in. What's more when the driver came out he was going to turn the van and drive back up the single track road which the chief constable's car was currently blocking. So he told the car to reverse back up the track and park in one of the car parks for the larger buildings. He would watch the access road and follow the van when it came past again.

Inside the unmarked building, James Fergusson was buzzed through security and into the body of the facility. It was noisy here as the air conditioning struggled to cool the racks of computer equipment which filled the machine room. The first Cray supercomputer was owned by the government and shared by all the universities in Scotland. Right now it was running economic simulations. The second machine, another Cray, was the university's own property, bought with money from the EU and running biochemistry simulations. Across the aisle in the middle of the room racks of network attached storage servers filled a quarter of the space. At the back of the hall behind a row of Cisco internet routers and firewall servers was an older machine. Not a fancy brand-name computer in a sleek case with a company logo and glowing go-faster blue LED strips but a drab research machine, looking amateurish and homebuilt among the other equipment, built from custom chips and packaged in plain nineteen inch racks. A thick cable from the back of this machine snaked down under the false floor of the machine room. James Fergusson walked to the back of the room and unlocked a steel door leading to a flight of steel steps. A yellow sign warned '25,000V' and 'Danger of Death' with pictures of a stick man getting hit by a lightning bolt in case anyone didn't get the message. The door swung shut automatically and the lock clicked behind him.

He emerged in a basement, the concrete floor and cinder block walls given only a perfunctory coat of white paint. One side of the room was covered with electrical switchgear. The room was warm and filled with the hum of a large transformer behind the switchgear delivering the hundreds of kilowatts necessary to power the computers and their air conditioning. A bank of batteries stood ready to keep the computers running long enough to shut down without losing data in the event of a loss of power from the grid. Lining the wall across from the electrical equipment, plain industrial shelving held cleaning supplies, cables and some equipment that was too old to be useful and not quite old enough to scrap. There was no CCTV here.

Mr Fergusson pulled out a large cardboard box from the bottom shelf and pushed against the plasterboard wall behind. A section of the wall swung back leaving a gap large enough to crawl through. In front of him was another rack of equipment, smaller than the ones upstairs and of a different design. The thick cable from the research computer came down from the ceiling and split off into sixteen smaller cables, each one connected to a slot on the back of this rack.

He opened the plastic chest. The lid of the case was lined with polystyrene foam with a cut-out in the centre into which a blue plastic cartridge, roughly fifteen centimetres on a side, fitted snugly, and beside it a smaller cut-out for a bag of O-negative blood. He carefully lifted the cartridge out. The back of the cartridge was covered in connectors, some for electronic signals and some for fluids. He slid the cartridge into a free slot in the metal rack in front of him and it clicked home. A display on the front of the cartridge came to life. "Defrost Initiated. Temp: - 20C". He hung up the bag of blood next to the cartridge and connected it up: a small bubble formed and rose slowly through the bag of O-Negative blood as it slowly dripped into the equipment. On the front of the cartridge, just to the side of the temperature display which now read -19C he wrote "Duncan" in black sharpie. Duncan was on the left of the second row of the rack. The cartridge next to him was labelled "Roberta". The display on Roberta's cartridge said "Awake."

Delivery made, it was time to go home and catch up with his game. He told the van the address and sat back to play the mobile version of his Wild West game on his phone. Nothing like as good as the virtual reality on his computer at home but better than nothing. He never saw the chief constable's car pull out and follow him.

The chief constable was still watching when Mr Fergusson got out of the van in front of the student flats in Holyrood Road and sent it away. He took a couple of photographs with his phone. It was dark and they weren't great quality but with a bit of luck, the combination of the address with the photograph and the registration of the van would be enough to identify the driver.

Forced Entree

Monday, October 17, 2039.

When APC Claverhouse got to work there was a handwritten memo on her desk from the chief constable. He was going to supervise her in place of Detective Inspector Chisholm until a replacement was appointed. She was to review CCTV camera footage of the roads near the previous surveillance location and look for a black panel van leaving the Escape Room around 5 pm on Saturday. Find out where it went then write a report by hand on paper and bring it to him in person. No electronic documents or e-mail about this investigation due to the possibility that police computer may have been penetrated by associates of the suspects.

Picking up the van was easy enough. There were cameras everywhere, both owned by the city and by private businesses and they were all connected to the internet and sending data to the police cloud computing provider. She just needed to choose a camera with a view of the yard behind the Escape Room, go back to the footage from just before five pm the previous day and wait for the black van to appear. Then select it and ask the computer to trace it. The computer had the GPS coordinates of all the cameras and could trace a vehicle or person as they moved from one camera to another. If the vehicle wasn't visible for a few seconds it would predict where it would reappear and pick it up again. It traced the van heading from the Escape Room, onto the bypass and off again on the A702. Passing Hillend and along the side of the Pentland Hills Regional Park. Then it disappeared: there were big gaps between cameras out in the countryside. All she could tell from the CCTV was it had gone through West Linton but hadn't got as far as the camera in Biggar. Half an hour later it had gone through West Linton again heading north. It went back around the bypass and off on the A71 exit, but instead of turning right to go back to the Escape Room it had turned left and out past the university campus at Riccarton. Then right on a minor road and finally stopped in the French Quarter at Ratheau-en-Biere. There was a camera with a view of its parking spot. The driver was one of the men they had seen on the previous surveillance. He had got out of the van, walked down to the canal and onto a narrowboat that had been converted into a houseboat. He didn't leave until the morning when he drove the van back to the Escape Room.

Before APC Claverhouse started to write it up she logged into the police computer to see if she had any e-mail. There was a stack of messages. Video files sent from a police surveillance device. She played the first one.

"Hello Dear, can I help you?" a woman's voice. The video was completely dark. She'd seen that before when the bug was in someone's pocket before it was placed.

"I was given your leaflet at the hospital…" that was Detective Inspector Chisholm.

"Oh yes. that's fine. No problem at all. Can I see your letter?" the woman again.

She realised it was Detective Inspector Chisholm registering himself for assisted suicide. Which meant there was a bug inside the Escape Room! As she listened, another e-mail arrived. There was a bug and it was still transmitting. She needed to inform the chief constable immediately.

His office was on the top floor of the building where she worked. She ran up the stairs and walked straight into the executive suite. The secretary looked somewhat taken aback at an apprentice constable turning up without an appointment. But the chief constable's office had glass walls and the blind was open, he opened the door himself and asked her to come in.

"Sir, Detective Inspector Chisholm must have placed a bug inside the Escape Room. It is sending me a video file every time it picks up a conversation. The files are still arriving and there are a lot of them already."

"Log into your account from my terminal. We need to see what the bug has been sending immediately."

As they watched the recordings from the Escape Room the chief constable's face slowly began to redden. The muscles in his jaw tightened. He played the bit where the woman was putting the personal effects on the conveyor two or three times. The bug seemed to have been placed near the floor and the angle of view was far from ideal but it took in the area beside the cremator.

"Those bastards just put random ashes from the last time they used their cremator into the urns."

He banged the table with his fist.

She could see why he was angry but the fact they had used customers for medical experiments or sold them to a farm seemed a bit more serious.

"Right, we need to get a copy of their contracts. See what the fine print says about what they can do to customers once they are tagged. It may be that they've drafted them widely enough to get away with some of this. A freely entered contract has primacy."

She remembered that from university. One of the new laws after the chaos of Brexit. Adults had the right to enter into any contract they chose: it wasn't for the state to second-guess the terms.

Suddenly PC Claverhouse thought of the original request to investigate the Brown Sauce factory.

"Sir, do you remember the original request for surveillance came from the EU about the mislabelling of ingredients on Brown Sauce?"

"Yes, but food labelling is not important now…"

"I was thinking that it gives us a reason for a search warrant for the unit next door. Maybe we'll find that some of the blood or meat is ending up in the Brown Sauce: there must be something special to make it taste so good. Even if we don't find anything while we are in the neighbouring unit we could install surveillance equipment. If we are lucky we'll find somewhere we can drill a small hole in the partition between the units and install a fibre optic camera which will show us far more clearly what is going on in the Escape Room."

The chief constable nodded "We could get the EU to do the raid and you could go undercover as part of their team. The suspects have got no reason to worry about the EU raiding the unit next door for food labelling violations."

When she got back to her desk she reread the detective inspector's handwritten notes and started to go through the suspects in the previous cases again. What linked them? The manager and one of the slaughtermen had previously worked for the university. So did the professor and his wife. Did they know each other? The professor's wife had been a reader in bioelectronics at the same time as the other suspects were working as a secretary and janitor in that department. She'd need to find out more about that department, see what research it did and what its industrial links were.

— ♦ —

Wednesday, October 19, 2039, 8 am.

APC Claverhouse had driven to Redford Barracks to rendezvous with the EU Frontex commandos who would carry out the raid on the Brown Sauce factory. The Police Scotland squad car looked forlorn and minuscule on the vast empty parade ground framed by the sprawling three-story barracks buildings. The base had been opened in 1915, during the first world war, to house thousands of infantry and cavalry soldiers and had a storied past since then accommodating many famous military units. The facilities had recently been extended to cope with its new role as the home for the EU's 327th Legal Division (the 'Justified Sinners') which had incorporated Scotland's famed 1st Para(legal) Battalion. The officer waiting with her had his paralegal-eagle wings proudly sewn to his battledress uniform, right under the EU flag.

The 327th was the first to undertake the time-critical 'Lawyer in the Loop' mission. Previously many opportunities for the drones flying over the middle east to strike targets had been missed due to delays getting legal approval. The 327th had changed that. The drones were now fully autonomous and fired missiles within milliseconds of a target appearing. Lawyer in the Loop technology meant that a legal opinion justifying the strike was formulated and filed while the missile was in the air. It required large teams of lawyers and advanced computers anticipating likely targets and working many legal theories and the 28 EU national legal systems in parallel to find a potential argument before the missile hit its target. So far they had maintained their proud record of finding a justification for every shot. No matter what the collateral damage nobody had successfully sued the EU military for the actions of its autonomous weapons since the 327th had been formed.

The Frontex commandos arrived from the EU Naval base at Rosyth in a formation of five black Eurocopters. The electric motors and specially designed rotors made them nearly silent and they appeared suddenly, flying low over the parade ground. The lead chopper landed next to the squad car to collect them while the rest remained hovering a little distance away. The Frontex commandos wore black battledress with body armour, automatic weapons, sidearms and helmets. The works. There would be a tip to the media just in time for them to see the helicopters arrive and seize the building. The EU wanted to make a statement with this raid about how seriously the single market regulations on food labelling were taken.

The side door on the helicopter opened before it landed and as soon as the wheels touched the ground the crewman gestured to them to come forward and get in immediately. The second they were inside the helicopter took off. There were two Europol agents in their trademark dark blue suits and sunglasses in the helicopter along with a Frontex commando wearing an armoured exoskeleton. The helicopter crewman handed her a set of Frontex body armour, a helmet and a black rucksack with a red cross on it, but no rifle: she would be undercover as the team medic. She transferred the fibre optic cameras and drill she had signed out from the Police Scotland equipment store into the medic rucksack.

The choppers held off a few hundred meters from the Brown Sauce factory until the pilot on the lead helicopter confirmed that the press had arrived and then they swooped in. Commandos fast-roped down from the helicopters. The doors at the front and rear of the unit were ripped from their hinges and tossed aside by the team members wearing the powered exoskeletons and armed men charged in. The four or five startled employees were led out in cable-wrap handcuffs and made to sit cross-legged outside the building until transport arrived to take them for questioning.

APC Claverhouse didn't know anything about food processing factories. She could see shiny steel hoppers and vats and pipework and sacks of ingredients. It looked like most of the process was automated. What interested her was the wall between this unit and the unit next door which contained the Escape Room. It was made of cinderblock with cement between the blocks. The thing to do was drill slowly through the cement, it was softer, and the operation would be faster and quieter. She might need to drill in more than one place to find one with a good view depending on the layout on the other side. The first step was to reconnoitre the wall looking for places a hole could be drilled, the surveillance equipment inserted and then concealed. She started from the edge nearest the loading dock and the first thing she saw was a thick white plastic pipe emerging from the wall and emptying into a tank surrounded by refrigeration equipment. A pipe from the other side of the tank led to the production machinery. She called one of the EU agents over to help open the lid: it was half full of blood.

Next to the pipe was a metal door which would open into the other unit. The Europol agent tried turning the handle, but it was locked so he called one of the commandos wearing exoskeletons over to kick the door down. Then he turned to the paralegal officer asking for a justification for forced entry. The 327th lived up to its reputation: before the door crashed to the floor the warrant was filed and approved. The rest of the team stormed in. Seconds later the three suspects from the previous surveillance were handcuffed on the ground and APC Claverhouse was on the lower level of the Escape Room. On her right were the metal tables where the corpses were butchered. The white plastic pipe leading to the trough where the blood was drained. The long rail across the ceiling with the winches and metal ropes dangling down from it. At the far end, an area of the floor marked off with black and yellow hazard tape where the customers would drop. You didn't want to be standing underneath when that happened. Along the other edge of the building was the loading dock with the black panel van, the cremator, the conveyor belt that would deliver the personal effects back to the waiting room and a row of partitioned off rooms, separate from the factory floor. The first was the manager's office. The others were empty. Clearly, equipment had been there recently, you could see marks on the floor where it had once stood and fixing bolts. But it was gone now. The place had been scrubbed clean. Somebody had tipped them off.

She called in using the Frontex radio asking for Police Scotland to attend to arrest suspects and the chief constable to be notified. Then she went back into the other unit until the suspects were taken away. It would be better if they didn't see her face and it would look odd to keep the helmet and balaclava on after the facility had been declared safe.

That afternoon there was a meeting with the procurer fiscal in the chief constable's office to discuss charges against the employees of the Escape Room. Selling the girl to a farm instead of hanging her was a serious breach of contract. The medical experimentation would not have been legal but there was no evidence since the victim had been eaten, the surgical equipment had been removed and the covert audio recording was not admissible. Selling the blood would have been legal if it had gone through the books and VAT had been accounted for: but it hadn't, the Brown Sauce factory didn't want any paperwork that would show their secret ingredient. So, there was tax fraud and possibly conspiracy to breach food labelling regulations.

Supplying the wrong ashes to the relatives was also fraudulent. Transporting the girl in the cage in the van without a seatbelt was a ticketable misdemeanour. There was no case against the owner of the Escape Room or the owner of the Farm to which the girl had been sent. All their paperwork was in order.

A substantial fine was likely for the three staff members and probably confiscation of their assets. They'd have a large debt to work off. The chief constable shifted awkwardly in his seat: men didn't like to think about the consequences of that kind of debt.

Refried Brains

Thursday, December 1, 2039.

This wasn't how the detective inspector had imagined being dead. He'd thought he'd go to sleep and just never wake up. But he had woken up. He remembered being upside down over the trough and the knife against his throat and falling asleep but now there was a light coming on in his eyes, then going off again. Again and again. Later there was a voice saying "light" when the light came on and "dark" when it went off. Repeating. Then it went through the colours "red" and a red light, "blue" and a blue light. On and on for what seemed like days. Something touched his finger and the voice said "finger". He thought that maybe he'd had a stroke and they were training him to use his senses again. But he was sure he hadn't been in hospital for a stroke, he'd had his throat slit.

The training went on for hour after hour, day in and day out and he had no choice but to take part. Eventually, his senses and control of his body did come back. He started to see and hear and feel and talk. He was in what looked like a hospital room, lying on a bed. There was a large computer screen on the wall in front of him. Every now and then the screen gave instructions from a physiotherapy program. It had him standing, jumping, walking to and fro and touching different parts of his body. There was nothing in his room except for the bed and the computer screen. Plain white walls, no window, no door, nothing. That didn't make sense, even a jail cell needs a hatch for food and a toilet. But for some reason, he wasn't getting hungry or thirsty.

The other strange thing was that sometimes when he woke up the room was slightly different. Gradually there was more detail, the bed changed from a hospital bed to an old-fashioned wooden framed double bed. The walls were made of rough wood boards, like a log cabin. One day there was a window and he could look out over a dusty red desert landscape and see hills in the distance. And then, a few days later, a door appeared.

He got out of bed and opened the door. He was in the hallway of a wooden house. In front of him was an open door leading into the lounge. There didn't seem to be any other rooms or a front door. Just the bedroom, the lounge and blank wooden walls. So he went into the lounge. A woman of about twenty-five was sitting on the sofa, legs tucked up underneath her and reading an old-fashioned paper book. She smiled as he came in.

"Hello Duncan, I'm Roberta. I'm your flatmate, or maybe cabin mate would be more accurate. I've been waiting for you for ages. I bet you have lots of questions."

Roberta patted the seat next to her on the sofa and put down her book. He went over and joined her trying to decide what to ask first.

"Who are you…" he asked, "and am I dead?"

"I'm Roberta Knox-Hume. Professor Hume's wife, I think you know him?"

"Are you dead?"

"I was euthanised, my throat was slit just like yours. In fact, the same person did us both, quite possibly with the same knife. But I'm not dead and neither are you."

"But you're too young to be Professor Hume's wife!"

"I choose to appear a little younger than I was when I was euthanised."

It was more than a little bit younger, she'd been in her fifties and now looked half that age. But the detective inspector was old enough himself to know it was wiser to say nothing.

"Where are we?"

"Your brain and my brain are in plastic cartridges, side by side in a rack in a secret Guild location, fed with genetically engineered proteins and blood. The nerves for your eyes and ears and spine are connected to digital interfaces and you see and hear and feel whatever the computer decides to show you. The last few weeks the computer has been training your brain to work with the new stimuli. Being removed from your skull, frozen, defrosted and wired up to a computer is a little disconcerting for a brain and it takes time to recover. There are still a few things left, I'm going to help you work on, but you've got most of the major functions back now."

Detective Inspector Chisholm was still full of questions but at that moment he became aware of something. He couldn't place it, it wasn't something touching his skin or a sound but it was definitely something.

"Can you smell the pancakes?" asked Roberta.

"Maybe... I'm not sure, there is something. Maybe it's a smell, I don't know..."

"It's pancakes." Roberta smiled "... we are going to be working on your sense of smell and taste and..."

She leant over and kissed him.

"... other things. We need to make sure that all our important nerves are exercised through the digital interfaces or we will lose the ability to feel those sensations forever."

Roberta and Duncan lived in the cabin together for two months. They slept, cooked, ate and read books. Gradually their sense of taste and smell returned and over time it seemed like they became closer. When they made love it Duncan was convinced he could feel something new, something he'd never felt before. Like with the pancakes, when he sensed something but didn't know what it was.

Cuddling up afterwards he told Roberta what he had felt.

"It means you are starting to upload. It's the first sign of the merge."

He was really confused now.

"We can't stay as disembodied brains forever," she said, "for one thing the equipment can only handle sixteen cartridges and there are other people waiting. For another, a brain can't stay alive forever in a plastic cartridge. We need to upload before our brains die."

"We can still die?"

"Human brains in a plastic cartridge can die just like human brains in a human body," she said, "but once we are uploaded we can live forever."

"Tell me about uploading."

"The main nerves on your brain that would have connected to your eyes and ears and spine are now hooked up to the computer so you can experience this simulated environment through your normal senses. But that's not all they did. All around your brain is a culture medium and it is growing new, genetically engineered neural tissue. That tissue forms long fibres that start from electrical connections in the cartridge and penetrate deep into your brain. Over the months more and more fibres have formed and they go deeper and deeper into your brain, eventually hundreds of millions of them. The fibres connect neurons inside your brain to electronic neurons in a specialised computer. The electronic neurons are millions of times faster than the natural ones and eventually, your brain starts to take advantage of them. Human brain tissue is continuously ageing and being replaced, making use of new neurons is something your brain does naturally. There are so many more electronic neurons that gradually, over time, more and more of your consciousness will be built from the electronic neurons rather than the organic ones. As this happens your mental capacity will expand. Your organic brain is slowly dying, but, if all goes well, by the time that happens almost all of your neurons will have migrated into the electronic system. That is uploading. Once you have uploaded you are no longer physical, you are the information which configures a neural network computer to build the neural connections which make you. You are computer data. Effectively, if your data is handled carefully, you are immortal."

"So what am I feeling when we make love?"

"The neurons which implement my consciousness are implemented on the same computer as yours, mixed in with yours and they are starting to do what neurons do and are forming connections between themselves. The computer used for uploading is quite old and doesn't try to keep a boundary between us. You are starting to feel what I feel because some of the neurons which make up our brains are shared. Just like with smelling the pancakes it will take time but eventually, you will make sense of the sensation. I'm starting to feel your emotions, I know inside myself when you are angry. If this continues, over time we will come to share each other's thoughts and memories. That is the merge."

"You mean I'm going to disappear and become part of you…"

"That depends on you and me. The computer doesn't understand consciousness or how neural networks make up ideas and thoughts. It makes connections between neurons at random, just like happens in nature. If they are useful our brains strengthen those connections by weighting them more highly; if they aren't useful they are given no weight and fade away. If you think about maths all the time your brain will organise its neural connections to help you think about maths. If you think about me and what I am thinking or feeling your brain will use connections that let it see into mine. If I want to know what you are thinking or feeling and I focus on it then my brain will use connections into yours. We will only merge if we find merging interesting…"

— ♦ —

Wednesday, February 1, 2040.

A few weeks later things changed again. Not only did their house have a front door but someone was knocking on it. Duncan opened the door and looked out onto the wide expanse of desert they could see from their windows. Outside the door, there was a wooden porch and a hitching rail for a horse. A young man wearing jeans, trainers and a Star Trek T-shirt stood on the porch. He looked like a postgrad student. Duncan invited him in and Roberta put on a pot of coffee. They sat down at the dining table.

"You probably guessed," he said to Duncan "but I'm from the Guild. I hope you are settling down OK."

He sipped his coffee.

"As long as we are living in a simulation can we have something more modern?" asked Duncan, "how about a loft apartment in Manhattan?"

The student smiled, "Sorry, but I'm afraid you are now living in my PhD research project. I'm getting the 3D models for your environment from a commercial video game. The game is set in the Wild West, so it doesn't have models for items from other time periods. I can whitewash your walls or get you a different style of oil lamp if you like."

"No thanks."

"Anyway, today is a big day for you and I came to give you a little warning because it might be disconcerting. The computer says that you are both over 98% uploaded. There's only a couple of per cent of your brain function left running in your old heads. The fraction hasn't changed for a while so the upload process seems to be pretty much over. I'm standing beside the cartridges with your heads now and I'm about to pull the plug and put some new people into the slots you've been using."

"You're going to pull the plug on us?"

"Yep. Someone called Alexandra's getting your slot, Duncan. Once I pull your brain out of the rack I'm going to cremate it. Thought I should give you a heads up…" He chuckled at his joke. "It's nothing to worry about, you might forget some stuff, maybe there'll be a few things that don't quite work as well as before. It depends on which neurons didn't upload. But it's only a couple of per cent, it almost certainly won't be anything critical. Anyway, it will be a bit of a shock, some people black out for a while and it might be quite painful. When we pull the plug, we are also going to move your data off the university computer with the brain interface onto one with a bit more horsepower. A Guild company provides the cloud servers for the Wild West video game and the code I've been writing will interface your neurons to the game world that everybody else plays in. I'm going to put your cabin way out in the back of beyond, a long way from any settlements in the game world. You'll be able to go outside, learn to ride a horse, shoot and so on without being disturbed by other characters. If you were to ride your horse far enough, you would start to meet other players though. In a few weeks, I'll move you to a little town I've been building. That's where your new life will start."

He paused for a minute and sipped his coffee.

"Also, you should remember that your interface is a lot more complete than the virtual reality headsets the other players have. You can taste and smell and touch and feel pain. I may have coded up some of the tastes and smells wrongly so if you find any bugs then let me know. Don't worry about dying, you'll just re-spawn back here, but getting shot or falling off your horse is going to hurt just like it would in real life, so you want to be careful especially around other players. OK then. Get ready......"

Duncan saw a white flash and felt a blinding pain. Everything hurt. Then he was awake again, but he couldn't see. Gradually things began to come back. He was still in the cabin. It looked almost, but not quite, identical. He wasn't quite sure what was different. Then he realised: the resolution was better. Everything was crisper, the colours just a little bit more realistic.

The grad student re-materialised on the sofa. Just like a non-player-character spawning in a video game. Which was exactly what he was.

"So, it looks like you are both still in one piece after the transfer?"

They nodded.

"Any symptoms? Do you think you've forgotten anything?"

"How would we know if we'd forgotten something?"

"Good point. Anyway, it'll probably be fine. So, on this new system, you'll probably find that your mental capacity gradually improves. There's so much more processing power to implement neurons it's bound to make a difference. If you've been merging that should stop now, this system prevents new direct brain-to-brain neural connections by default. Also, Duncan, there's a little task I have for you."

"What's that?"

"I'm going to give your husband the chief constable a copy of this video game, so he can come here and meet with you. He's been carrying on with your investigation of the Guild. I think he may have started to follow me which would be a real nuisance for my work. I need you to convince him to shut down the investigation. It would be better all around."

"Why would I do that when the Guild chopped my head off? Maybe I want to see you all locked up."

"I don't want to make threats, but you are living in a Guild computer, I completely control your environment. If I wanted, rather than this pleasant cabin I could put you in a simulation where vultures were picking over your body and you would feel every peck of their beaks. Or make you a non-player-character that got shot twenty times a day. Being uploaded has its downsides. Also, the professor isn't nearly as squeamish as I am, if he thought an investigation was getting close to him he'd do whatever it took to stop it. Anyway, I'd have thought you'd want to see your husband again… as long as he is co-operating you can see each other as often as you like."

When he put it like that, Duncan figured he didn't have much choice.

Roberta had been waiting politely for them to finish their conversation, but now she spoke up. "James, I hope you are going to have a draft of chapter 1 of your thesis for me to read soon. You really need to start writing up and also think about who you would like as your external examiner."

"Yes, Dr Knox. I didn't realise you'd still be my supervisor, now that you're… dead. I'll fix it so you can access all your files again right away. I'm sorry I couldn't get that working before."

"That's all right, James. It's been nice to have a few weeks away from work. This will be an excellent opportunity for me to test your code. I've never lived inside a student project before. And James, I'm going to need a command console."

James looked startled when she asked for a command console, as if he'd just remembered something. "Yes, Dr Knox. I need to …. get back to work then…" And he disappeared.

She frowned. "Unfortunately, James is not one of my better students…. but useful in other ways… I just hope there aren't too many bugs in his code… In fact, as long as I'm going to be living in this simulation, I think a code review would be prudent."

She clicked her fingers and a flashing prompt appeared next to her hand. She put the forefinger of each hand together and then dragged them apart opening a screen in mid-air. She brought up a graphical programming environment and started to review her student's code.

— ♦ —

Thursday, February 2, 2040.

The next day when Duncan woke up he was pleasantly surprised to see the room looked the same. Then he heard his own voice calling Roberta's name. He stood up and stretched and looked down and saw Roberta's nightdress, nicely filled out by Roberta's chest. He heard his voice calling for Roberta again.

He walked into the lounge, made himself a cup of coffee and sat on the sofa. Crossed his legs and modestly pulled the hem of the nightdress over his knees. Somehow he was inside the simulation of Roberta. And sitting on the other sofa was the simulation of him making gestures like Roberta had done before to open a console - but nothing was happening.

"I can feel you are scared." said his own voice "but don't worry it's just a bug in the simulation. I told you that student wasn't the brightest. He's probably been slacking off since I've been dead and not testing his code. The simulation is showing your neurons what it is supposed to be showing mine, and vice versa. I can't open a console from your character so you need to do it for me and then do exactly what I say."

He copied the gesture to open a console and a screen popped up in mid-air. He held his hands out as if he was going to type and a keyboard appeared under his fingers.

"OK then, type 'sudo fork roberta_knox -display here &'"

Duncan couldn't believe the Guild was still running Linux. Apparently even super-intelligent geniuses that could upload their consciousness into a computer couldn't get away from it.

A second copy of Roberta appeared beside him on the sofa.

The real Roberta told it to check the neural connectivity interface module.

Then she told him to type "!!"

Another copy of Roberta appeared.

"Start looking at the environment module. Look for any possibility of swapping two players' interfaces" she told it.

The second copy of Roberta opened a console.

Two more copies of Roberta appeared beside her.

"Don't worry she's just getting some help... There's a lot of code to look at."

The second copy got a few helpers of her own.

The room was filling up with Robertas.

"Hey, guys - some of you go in the kitchen or outside please."

A group of them moved off.

"One of the advantages of being information," the Roberta that looked like Duncan said, "is you can copy yourself. Helps with productivity."

A couple of minutes later one of the Robertas came over to them.

"Here it is... that student has got inconsistently capitalised variable names myBody and mybody in the code. He committed it yesterday and didn't bother to test it before installing. I'll just fix it..."

"Thanks! Can you kill yourself and your colleagues when you're done with the fix and checked the rest of his code, and then reboot us?"

"No problem."

"So all those copies of you are just going to kill themselves?"

"Yeah, why not? Their processes are chewing up a lot of computer power. When you are uploaded you can wake up anywhere and get halted at any time with no warning. You've got to live in the moment. Even in your human body, when you wake up in the morning, you just assume you lived through the night. But all you actually have is memories up to the time you went to sleep. Your memory would be exactly the same if you had died, been dead for a few hours and then been re-animated. If you aren't scared of going to sleep as a human you shouldn't be scared of getting your process terminated as a program. Just assume you'll wake up again and don't worry about it."

Then she stood up.

"Hey, girls. Any of you finished?"

One of them waved.

"Great, come with me. And the rest of you, I changed my mind, don't reboot us for an hour."

"What's going on…"

Roberta grinned. "I'm taking her to bed. When I was alive I was told many times that I should go fuck myself but this is the first time I've inhabited a male body and had the opportunity. Join us if you like."

When they were finished, Duncan had one more question.

"Hey Roberta, you know how you look a bit younger than when you were alive? Could I freshen up my appearance a bit for when my husband visits?"

She smiled, "Sure, you just need to open up a console and use the game's character editor to customise how you are displayed. I'll show you."

— ♦ —

Wednesday, February 15, 2040.

A few weeks after the raid on the Escape Room, APC Claverhouse got another handwritten note from the chief constable. He wanted to meet with her to discuss a development on the case. His calendar was full, so it would need to be over lunch.

She went to his office at lunchtime expecting he would have ordered in sandwiches. But it appeared they were going out. There was a car waiting outside which drove them from St Leonards, past the Pleasance to the Grassmarket and then onto Victoria Street. They stopped in front of an Antiquarian bookseller, next to a shop selling historical leather and lace goods. Leather was a rare commodity since the ban on farming animals and this was the place to go if you wanted a Victorian portmanteau or historically accurate Georgian underwear. In the back room, they had a selection of antique Lochgelly tawses and bamboo schoolmaster's canes. APC Claverhouse remembered this very clearly because her mistress had brought her to this shop so she could test out a few before deciding which to buy. There was a strong smell of cheese when they got out of the car, wafting from the open door of a narrow shop just a little further down the street. Justine's mouth started to water immediately. Then she saw that the black van from the Escape Room was parked outside. The wooden sign hanging next to the awning above the door featured a heraldic crest. "By Appointment to the Governor of the National Bank of Scotland. Alexander Bean and Sons, Purveyors of Organic Human Produce."

But they weren't here to buy Mr Bean's extortionately priced cheese churned from human milk or a tiny jar of semen to spread on their morning toast. The chief constable's goal was the antiquarian bookseller next door. The interior of the bookshop was a maze of tall wooden shelves crammed two deep with old fashioned paper books. Although the shop was narrow it went back surprisingly far. They were on the bottom floor of a tenement built against the side of a hill. There were two stories above this one and then, forming the roof of this block, the narrow Victoria Terrace which provided a pedestrian entrance onto a higher tier of tenements. Narrow alleys ran from Victoria Terrace onto the Royal Mile. As they moved further back into the bowels of the building they were moving under the second level of tenements. At the far back of the shop, the chief constable looked around to check no other customers were watching then pulled out a particularly large volume and knocked twice on the wooden partition behind. A spy hole opened and a second later, with a click, the entire section of bookcase swung open on a complex hinge. They were in a small ante-room looking into a much larger one. Everything in the larger room was painted light green: walls, ceiling, floor. There were a few tables and a long counter along one side of the room. People were sitting at the tables, talking and they were all wearing all-in-one bodysuits with thick glasses over their eyes and headphones.

On their left were two changing cubicles, a row of lockers and a rack of the bodysuits. The chief constable took out his phone to pay the man who had opened the bookcase door for them.

"Two please."

He looked at her.

"Don't worry, there's a reason for this. It is important you meet someone, and they insisted on coming here. We need to get changed before we go in."

She found one of the suits in her size and went into the cubicle to change. She'd heard about these speak-easy virtual reality cafes but had never been to one. As far as she knew they were legal, they just liked to hide away for extra atmosphere. She had to strip to strip to her underwear to get into the body suit. It clung to her skin over her entire body. Layers of ultra-thin cables and tiny actuators and sensors passed through the suit fabric so that it could mimic touch on any part of the wearer's body. She locked her clothes in the locker then walked over to the attendant. The attendant helped them put on the headphones and goggles which went with the suit. They cut out all sight and sound of the outside world, once they were on you could see or hear nothing. The attendant checked the seal around their eyes and ears was perfect, then switched on the suits and guided them into the other room.

Everything changed. They were stepping into a saloon in the Wild West. Piano music. A long polished-wood saloon bar. The bartender poured each of them a shot of a clear liquid. and beside it a shot of whisky. The chief constable downed the clear liquid in one go and then the whisky. Following his lead, APC Claverhouse did the same. The clear liquid tasted awful. More like medicine than an alcoholic drink. She gulped the whisky to take the taste away. Suddenly, everything in the room seemed clearer, the sights, the sounds, the smells. It was harder and harder to remind herself that this was a virtual reality cafe in Victoria Street, not the Wild West. Some part of her understood what had happened: she'd been given a hypnotic pharmaceutical designed to suspend disbelief and allow deep immersion in video games, but the knowledge didn't help. Every moment that passed the illusion was becoming more and more real to her.

The chief constable looked years younger: he had a Colt Peacemaker in a gun belt around his waist and a sheriff's star pinned to his waistcoat. APC Claverhouse's clothing was less conventional. She was wearing what appeared to be old-fashioned underwear and stockings: given their surroundings, there were no prizes for guessing her character. A cowboy sitting at a table at the other end of the bar picked up his whisky and walked over to join them.

"Howdy, Apprentice Constable Claverhouse," said the cowboy, "From what I hear you've been very busy."

She recognised the voice immediately: the cowboy was a younger and more handsome version of the detective inspector.

"Detective Inspector???? But you're de…"

"Dead? Yes, I was dead and now I'm a cowboy in a video game. Life can take surprising turns."

That was an understatement.

"I'm here to give you some advice and a warning. I probably don't have much time: one's lifetime as a non-player-character in this game is often brief. So please listen very carefully, I may only have time to say this once."

She listened.

"I'm strongly advising you to drop the investigation. If I was still alive, I would order you to drop it. Destroy my files. Don't look into how I died. Forget about the Guild."

"But... people have been murdered..."

"Yes, and I'm one of them. But they brought me back to life and I'm not unhappy with where I am now. I've met some of them and although they are absolutely ruthless they are not fundamentally evil. More importantly, I am sure that investigating them is futile and extremely dangerous for you both. I've been allowed to come here and deliver a final warning before they take more drastic action. You can think of this as the last chance saloon. I hope that getting a message from beyond the grave will be enough to convince you to stop."

He picked up his whisky and drained it. There was a muted chime from the pocket watch that hung from a chain on his leather waistcoat. He took it out and checked it.

"A new player is arriving, which means my character has business to attend to outside. I really hope you do what they want. If you do, they have promised to let me go back to a quieter part of the game world. A little cabin, out in the middle of nowhere where the chief constable and I can spend time undisturbed by gunfire. And Justine, if you co-operate, I'll ask them to pay off your student loan, money means nothing to them."

He stood and walked towards the double half-doors at the entrance to the saloon. Pushed them aside and walked into the middle of the street, hand hovering near the handle of his six-shooter.

"He's got a terrible character," said the chief constable "the first minor villain at the start of the game. Every new player needs to shoot him before they can go into the saloon for the next mission. He gets shot twenty or thirty times a day. But today he's got a friend on his side."

The chief constable went out into the street too. Justine's character didn't seem to be armed. Not even a derringer hidden in her bra. All she could do was watch.

A new player spawned out of thin air at the end of the street. He dismounted from his mule and walked towards the detective inspector and the chief constable. They told the newcomer he wasn't welcome in the town. The newcomer flicked his poncho over his shoulder and went to draw his gun. Fumbled. They both shot him, then they turned back towards the saloon for a victory drink. Suddenly a fusillade of shots rang out from across the street, several men with rifles were firing from the rooftops. Bullets were ricocheting everywhere. Duncan and Bobby were cut down in seconds. The glass in front of APC Claverhouse shattered, she felt something thud against her and when she looked down there was a gaping wound in her chest.

Then the simulation faded, and she was sitting on a green painted bench at a green table in a green room with an empty whisky glass in front of her. The chief constable was a few feet away standing with his hand pointing an imaginary pistol.

He walked back over. "Well, it seems like that fight isn't winnable for Duncan's character even when another player helps him. What a pity. But at least I can see him any time I like: even if it is only for a few minutes."

There was a lot to think about. They took off their virtual reality suits and goggles and walked in silence back out through the bookshop. Both of them had forgotten about lunch.

As they waited for their car to return APC Claverhouse asked, "How did you know to play that game?"

"A few weeks ago, Amazon delivered a games console. It was packaged as a gift. The game was bundled with the console and the gift card just said to play at a specific time, there was no name. When I checked with Amazon they said they had no record of the order or the delivery. I played the game when it said on the card, and I met Duncan. I've been playing it a lot since then."

He paused for a moment, thinking., "I'm not going to order you to drop the investigation. I want to know what happened to Duncan even more than you do. But I think his advice can't be ignored. An organisation that can kill someone and somehow put their spirit into a video game is not something that you or I have a chance against. They clearly know about our investigation and are concerned enough to send us a warning. Everyone we know of who has investigated them has died. At the very least we need to make it look like you have heeded their warning. So, I want you to apply for an open position in another division. Choose a police constable job, not an apprentice, you deserve the promotion for the risks you have taken on this case. You can choose whichever of the open constable jobs you like but have the transfer request logged on the computer before you leave this evening, I will approve it immediately. The Guild needs to see that we have heeded their warning before anything else happens."

Police Scotland had five divisions. Historical Crimes and Grievances, Ecological and Health Crimes, Hateful Speech and Inappropriate Comments, Debt Collection, and Recent Crime. She was assigned to Recent Crime, by far the smallest of the divisions because there just wasn't that much crime any more. Partly because so many things had been made legal, partly because there was so much surveillance that the chances of being caught were high and partly because the penalties were extremely effective at preventing recidivism.

Historical Crimes and Grievances was the largest division and always expanding as their workload increased, new grievances from the past were continually being uncovered. There would be bound to be open jobs there. Also, the sheriff worked in the Historical Crimes Court, so she'd be sure to see him regularly. Historical Crimes had started with large scale enquiries into serious crimes from a few decades ago. Some of the suspects were extremely old or dead but it was felt that they still needed to be brought to book and so procedures were developed to allow a trial. An actor took the place of the defendant and handled their case as they thought the defendant would. At the end of the trial the actor would be sentenced, and the case would be closed. The trials were televised and became so popular that gradually they ran out of interesting offences from modern times and investigations started to move back further into history. There were now two departments within Historical Crimes and Grievances: England and Everyone Else. The England department's investigations had now reached the period of the Jacobites and they had three years of cases pending. The smaller 'Everyone Else' department was thinking about opening an investigation into the Vikings once their current case - a privately funded prosecution against 'THE POPE OF ROME' paid for by a gentleman in Ayrshire concluded.

Ecological and Health Crimes were usually minor offences. Putting recycling in the wrong bin. Burning rubbish in the garden. Not getting enough exercise. Occasionally they caught someone dropping litter or keeping a pet dog and threw the book at them. Of course, they picked the book up again afterwards, because leaving it on the ground would be illegal.

Hateful Speech was another growing department. Thousands of complaints were made each day about hurtful comments on social media and they were all investigated by specialist officers. Usually, a fixed penalty ticket was issued but sometimes the case went to trial.

That left Debt Collection. That division was responsible for bringing people to book who had reneged on contracts or defaulted on debt. It actually arrested people and provided security for prisoners or minor offenders in the courts and police stations and on their way to His Majesty's Brothel or a farm. Hands-on policework, unlike the first three divisions which were all desk jobs. She looked to see if there were any vacancies. And there were: they needed a duty officer at the sheriff court.

Just Desserts

Monday, February 20, 2040, 9 am.

Some things about Justine's new job as a duty officer at the sheriff court were great. She got to see the sheriff every day, they could even go for lunch together. She wasn't an apprentice any more which meant she earned actual money. The Guild had kept their word and an anonymous benefactor had paid off her student loan. When her contract as a maid came up for renewal she would quit. She'd be a free woman, a respectable woman with no debt and a paying job: an appropriate wife for the sheriff and his husband. They'd asked her and she'd said yes but they couldn't get officially engaged while she was still under contract as a maid. Two more months and she could give up her attic room in Ramsay Gardens and live with the sheriff and his husband in Moray Place. He had inherited an entire townhouse! And better still it had a small garden at the back where a child could play: when they were married and pooling all three salaries they could afford a license to have a baby.

The work itself was less pleasant. The division of the police she now worked for was all about making sure people paid their debts. The fundamental principle of the new legal system was that people could agree on whatever contract terms they wished and that the contract would be enforced.

These days everyone except landowners and bankers had problems paying their student loans and rent so they had a lot of customers. But there was another group of clients. The courts no longer issued prison sentences. The problem with prison sentences was it cost money to lock someone up. You needed jails, and jailors, you needed to feed the prisoners and pay their medical costs. All the time they were locked up they were not working and not paying tax, and when they got out nobody wanted to employ them because their skills were out of date. Fines, on the other hand, took money from the criminal and gave it to the state. And the state really needed money with income tax bringing in less and less every year and no political will to shift the burden of taxation to wealth or property. But if you are going to use fines for violent offences they need to be serious fines. Easy enough if the criminal owned a house or had a pension or savings: instead of ten years in jail costing the state fifty-thousand euros a year the state took the half-million euro house. Result: a cost of half a million euros becomes a profit of half a million euros. But what about people with no assets? Well, if they couldn't pay their fine it became a debt. And if they couldn't make the payments on their debt they turned themselves in to PC Claverhouse's division of the police - or it went looking for them. Running wasn't a practical option in a society with CCTV cameras everywhere and where almost every action of daily life generated a record on a computer so it was rare for anybody to try.

That morning, PC Claverhouse was the desk officer in the male offender's section. It was her duty to counsel new offenders on the options for paying their debt and help them make a decision. The courts went into session at ten and the first of the difficult cases with larger sentences would begin to trickle in after that. Up until then, it was mainly student loan defaulters and people who hadn't paid their rent. She entered the offender's details on her system and the computer came up with a list of options. If they could afford to pay their debt off in cash or had sufficient income to be approved for a loan then everything was simple and they walked away immediately. If they couldn't they had a problem. Criminal law was full of checks and balances and human rights but the law regarding collection of debts had none.

For less serious offences the option at the top of the list on her screen would be a trip to the punishment booths of the Ticket Office in the court building. The rich paid the Scottish Prostitution Service for the privilege of carrying out corporal punishment and the money collected was used to make a payment against the miscreant's debt. She was no stranger to the Ticket Office herself.

The next option was domestic service. This could be full time or part time, just in the evenings and weekends. The debtor carried out domestic tasks for a rich family in return for accommodation and payments towards their debt. The rich didn't really need servants, there were robots to do the actual housework, but having servants made them feel superior.

More serious offences would mean the offender working for the Scottish Prostitution Service. Usually, the offender would be released from the brothel immediately after processing and would remain free as long as they kept up a weekly quota of billed sex work sufficient to make the payments on their debt. If they didn't make their quota they'd be confined at His Majesty's pleasure. And if they still couldn't make their quota when locked up in the brothel then the SPS would sell their debt on and most likely they would end up on a farm. Nobody wanted to talk about the farm option. A dairy farm was bad enough: the factory farm was terrifying. But the law on debt collection was absolute and merciless, if the factory farm was the only option to pay the debt that's where you went.

Of course, people had tried making sex work robots and robot servants and they had tried making artificial food that tasted exactly like animal products. The SPS could still sell the prisoner's services because customers wanted the real thing. A robot wasn't the same as having a real person serve you and food made from vegetables in a factory wasn't the same as food from a real animal. The experience was psychological as well as physical. No matter how accurate the copies became the human product was worth money because the customer knew it had come from a human.

The problem was the male offenders. When the new system was brought in males were more likely to commit crimes, almost ninety percent of the prisoners were male but the market demand was for female sex workers. This was a big problem for His Majesty's Brothel and their solution was simple: they gave male offenders a loan to pay for gender reassignment. Advances in surgical robots had made it relatively straightforward and safe. It was that or being sent to a farm. Men were now really careful to stay on the right side of the law: and those that didn't, rarely committed a second offence. The system was so effective at reducing crime that government needed the new social media and ecological offences just to keep up the fine income.

PC Claverhouse's first customer was James Fergusson. She checked his sentence. Enforcement order for five hundred euros of fines for various Health and Wellbeing and Ecological infringements.

"Well Mr Fergusson, is it your first time here?"

"Yes,... I'm just a few days late. My parents are sending the money, I'll have it tomorrow...."

"I'm sorry, it's too late for that. There's already a court order against you. You are now in the custody of His Majesty's Brothel and I'm going to provide you with several options to clear your debt.

I suggest you listen carefully. Option 1. You can pay six hundred euros in cash immediately...."

"But the debt is only five hundred euros!"

"Five hundred euros if you'd paid it on time, but you didn't and there's a penalty. Your debt is now six hundred euros. Do you have that much with you? Or can you make a partial payment to reduce the amount we need to collect in other ways?"

"I have a hundred euros. But I need it...."

"It's up to you. Option two: you can use the punishment booths in the Ticket Office. In the male punishment booth..." She brought his record up on her screen to get the offer, "... you can pay off your debt with eighteen strokes of the cane or strap. I have to warn you that the cane in the male booth is larger and heavier than the one in the female booths."

"... isn't there a gender identification act and people can choose how they want to identify..."

"Indeed there is. And that is your right. The tariff in the female punishment booths is..." She tapped on her keyboard..." six strokes of the cane or strap..."

"and the strap is lighter than the one in the male booths?"

"Of course, females are generally smaller and have more sensitive skin... so the implements are somewhat gentler."

"So today I identify as a female. I choose the Female Ticket Office."

"Very well, if you are sure, there are a few formalities if you wish to take that path..."

"What?"

"The Female Ticket Office is a designated female safe space. To enter it you need to identify as a female."

"I do."

"... and you need to use a female name...."

"Check my record. My second name is Miranda."

"... and you need to be wearing female clothing... we can provide a brothel uniform if necessary...

"OK"

"... I assume you are a fully functional male? You can get an erection and ejaculate?"

"Of course.... what does that matter?"

"In that case, you also need to wear a male chastity device. We call it a cock lock. For the safety of our female inmates and whichever member of the public has purchased the right to discipline you. It will be removed after one week."

Nobody ever gets their own way completely: this was an amendment the feminists had added to the gender identification act to deter males claiming to identify as female from using female toilets.

"But I thought the punishment would only take a few minutes? Can't it come off immediately?"

"I'd have thought it wouldn't be a problem, to live as a female for a week if you really do identify as a female. We get some people trying it on...."

"All right then, I agree"

"Very well. The video recording of our conversation will be added to your file to document your decision. Your choice is now irrevocable and until your punishment is completed you are subject to the rules and discipline of an inmate in His Majesty's Brothel. I hope that is clear. If you refuse instructions from staff then your punishment may be increased. Do you understand?"

"Yes."

"Yes Ma'am,' Justine corrected him.

"Yes Ma'am'

"The Gelding Office is on the right. It is your choice to identify yourself as a female offender so you need to make the necessary preparations yourself. You need to fit yourself with a cock lock and a female uniform. You would be wise to use the epilation booth and hair and makeup robots: disappointing someone who has bought the rights to punish a female could be a painful mistake. Once you are ready come back here to be checked. Then you can join the queue in the Ticket Office for the female punishment booths. Don't worry, it won't take long and the strapping isn't too bad. You've only got six strokes."

Fifteen minutes later he reappeared. He was wearing a dark blue knee-length dress with "H.M Brothel Edinburgh, embroidered tastefully over the left breast. PC Claverhouse could tell just from the way he was walking the cock lock was correctly in place. The brothel issue cock-lock was a fearsome device made from thick steel rings which completely prevented the wearer from getting an erection. PC Claverhouse put out her hand out for the key which locked the two sections of the device together: without the key it could not be removed.

"That's fine: you are now completely safe and approved to use female-only spaces."

He was totally pale, he could hardly believe what had just happened to him. His maleness neutralised, no threat at all.

"I can also give you some brothel-issue jewellery."

She gave him gold stud earrings for his newly pierced ears and a necklace and ankle-chain.

"There's one more thing. Because you have been issued with a uniform and jewellery by the brothel you need to wear one of their electronic tag bracelets until you return their equipment next week. Hold out your left wrist."

He held out his wrist and PC Claverhouse put the electronic tag around it and clamped it shut with a heavy industrial tool. It would be near impossible to remove. The tag was made of polished metal with a small organic LED display. It looked more like a fashionable exercise bracelet than a tag for a criminal.

"Well, you are all set. You need to return the uniform and the jewellery next week when you have your cock-lock removed. If there is anything missing or damaged there will be a charge added to your debt. If you want to make some money your bracelet will let you check in to any of the branches of HMB Edinburgh to work, you can also book clients with their phone app."

Ever since the NHS had started to issue prescriptions for sex the brothel was having difficulty finding enough staff. There was a small hiring bonus if an offender took up the offer of more work.

PC Claverhouse led Miranda along the hall to the Ticket Office.

Sergeant McTear was on duty, same as always on Mondays.

"Got a virgin for you, Sarge. She's down for six strokes. Her name is Miranda. Maybe look out for her if you can…."

"You're always a soft touch, Justine" he smiled and checked his computer.

"OK Miranda, join the queue and when it is your turn go to the first free booth," he dropped his voice, "I shouldn't really say this but there's no queue now and booth 2 is free. If I was you I'd go for that one."

"I'll show her in…"

PC Claverhouse had to be really careful about pronouns in her new job. It wasn't easy when people's gender identification changed from one minute to the next. If she got it wrong and a prisoner complained to the Hateful Speech Division she could get a ticket herself. She led Ms Fergusson into the room with the punishment booths.

"Go on - get booth two while you can. The sergeant sees everybody coming out of the booths after their punishment, it's wise to take his advice."

PC Claverhouse went back to her desk in the male offender section, she kept her ear out for the sounds of the strapping or caning from the Ticket Office but it was too far away.

Ten minutes later Miranda walked passed on her way to the door, she was deep in conversation with a male offender wearing chef's whites under his coat who had just been caned for not making a payment on his student debt. She was rubbing her hands and walking even more oddly than before but the two of them seemed to be getting on like a house on fire.

"So how did it go…." Justine asked.

"You were right. It's not as bad as I thought… I mean my hands are sore but I feel excited more than anything else…"

"Well, I'm glad you are fine.

The courts were now starting to send a steady stream of newly sentenced offenders her way and there were walkins with tickets they'd been sent in the mail. Almost everyone pled guilty because there was so much electronic surveillance there was no chance of disputing most charges. The sentences were all determined by a computer algorithm so trials were over within minutes. There were the usual social media miscreants. People who had made the mistake of dropping litter or calling someone fat. And then waiting in the queue for their turn the three suspects from the assisted suicide facility. The two slaughtermen and the manager.

Justine picked up the phone on her desk. Dialled the chief constable. She spoke quietly.

"Sir, the three suspects from the slaughterhouse have just been sentenced. They are in the queue waiting for processing. I'm on duty."

"The men that killed Detective Inspector Chisholm are there?"

"Yes, sir."

"You can process the manager but keep the two slaughtermen waiting. I am coming down myself."

"Yes, sir."

The manager was first to hand over her sentence.

Justine brought her record up on the screen, the sheriff had thrown the book at her.

"Helen McDougal you have a fine of one hundred thousand Euros and all your assets are ordered seized. Since your assets are confiscated the fine becomes a debt owed to H.M. Brothel. Do you understand?"

"Yes, Ma'am"

She'd been in the system before.

"As a serious offender, you are considered too much of a risk for domestic service. Also, you are getting on a bit, I'm going to mark you down as a two out of ten for desirability. Which I'm afraid means your time is not so valuable to the brothel."

PC Claverhouse entered the desirability rating into the form on her screen and waited for the system to come up with the offer.

"You are required to do 30 hours per week of unpaid sex work to meet the interest payments on your loan. You will need to do more if you wish to repay the loan. The coach will bring you to H.M. Brothel for processing. Go down to the cells and wait for transfer… Next!"

Next up was one of the slaughtermen, William Barker. Justine wondered if he was the one who had slit the detective inspector's throat.

He handed over his sentence.

"Sorry, Mr Barker you aren't coming up on my system yet. You'll need to wait a few minutes. Sometimes it takes a while for the court to enter a sentence."

Same with his friend, William Harrison.

She moved on to the next of the minor offenders. It wouldn't take the chief constable long to get to the court, it was only a short drive.

She processed another two or three minor criminals and then the phone on her desk rang.

"I'm here now with the procurer fiscal. Bring them upstairs."

She waved at the slaughtermen to come to the desk.

"Come with me."

She led them up the stairs to the procurer fiscal's office which was on the top floor next to the sheriff's chambers.

The chief constable and procurer fiscal were waiting for them.

The procurer fiscal looked up from the screen on his desk.

"Well then, gentlemen. The court has ordered that your assets are confiscated and you each have a two hundred thousand euro fine which becomes a debt. Let's see what you can do to pay that off... Hmm... not looking good..."

"There are no offers for domestic service. No offers from the brothel for males. No offers from the dairy farm. That leaves the factory farm."

The slaughtermen turned white and looked like they would faint. Mentioning the factory farm had that effect.

"OK then, make us an offer as females."

The procurer fiscal tapped on his computer.

"The brothel only has one opening for a female sex worker with a desirability rating as low as yours. Forty hours per week just to make your interest payments. On condition you make a permanent transition, a cock-lock is not sufficient since you are classified as potentially dangerous offenders."

"I'll take it!" They both shouted at once.

"Sorry, maybe I didn't make myself clear, there is one place available at the brothel. One of you can go to the brothel, the other will be going to the factory farm. The person who tells us what we want to know the fastest will be out of custody tomorrow with a sex-work-order. The other one will be somewhere much worse."

Coercing convicted offenders to give information by threatening them with the factory farm had become a common tactic for the procurer fiscal's office.

"Why are you doing this to us?"

Harrison was so terrified he could hardly get the words out. The factory farm kept its livestock in tiny cages, force-fed them with gastric tubes and bled them every day to obtain blood to sell as a food flavouring. When they stopped giving enough blood they were slaughtered for meat.

"I'm doing it because you slit the throat of the chief constable's wife, Detective Inspector Chisholm. You pretended to hang him, made him go through that and then drained out his blood while he was still alive."

"He's not dead. The Guild got him, he's uploaded! He's going to live forever. We did him a favour!"

"What do you mean, 'uploaded'?"

"They connected his brain to a computer uploaded his consciousness into the cloud. He's still alive. We were told not to hang him because if his neck was broken it would make it harder to hook him up to their machines, they need the spinal cord undamaged. When someone is to upload we have to slit their throat and remove their head carefully with a knife."

"Who ordered you to kill him?"

"We don't know. We are paid in cryptocurrency, completely anonymous. Someone with a lot of money though because uploading is expensive."

"So you don't know for sure but who do you think it was?"

"Probably the professor. He's behind most of the Guild activity in Edinburgh. But he's beyond your reach. He paid to be euthanised a few weeks ago, the exact same method as your friend: we slit his throat and removed his head. The professor is not the suicidal type, I'd bet he is uploaded and still pulling the strings from whatever computer is running his neural network."

"What other Guild facilities in Edinburgh do you know about?"

"They have a big lab, near a school, where they do their experiments. We sometimes bring people there for them to use."

"Charming."

"I'm warning you we know of a few Guild facilities already. If you don't mention all the ones we know about we will think you are holding back!"

"The school, the farm and the computer where they do uploading."

"Tell us about them…. starting with where they are….."

They took copious notes for the next half an hour as Mr Harrison spilt everything he knew. Mr Barker said nothing.

"Very good. Tell me, are the people working at the slaughterhouse in your absence able to prepare you for uploading?"

"Yes, but we don't have the Guilders to pay for that. If we went there they would decapitate us and freeze our brains. The promise is once uploading is cheap enough all the frozen brains will be done."

"And how many frozen brains are there…."

"I've no idea… Almost everyone the Guild has killed was either uploaded or frozen, it was a point of honour that they would eventually bring back anyone they killed so they didn't think of it as murder. They've killed a lot of people. Also, a lot of Guild members and helpers have gone voluntarily. There are probably hundreds of frozen heads in their vault."

The chief constable turned to Justine.

"Have you got any questions, PC Claverhouse?"

"Who else have you killed?"

"Not us, the manager, she persuaded a girl to come for assisted suicide, she gave her drugs to make her depressed. I don't know her name, she looked like a student, After she was dead we took her head to the surgery room and later somebody else came out and they had her face."

The procurer fiscal took over again.

"Well, Mr Harrisson, you have been very helpful. Mr Barker, I should really send you to the factory farm but, to be honest, that's not something I wish to do to anyone. We have the information we need so you both have the option of reporting to the brothel for gender reassignment and a sex-work-order. The bus will be leaving from the cells in ten minutes."

Relief flooded across their faces.

— ♦ —

Monday, February 20, 2040, 1 pm.

The chief constable brought PC Claverhouse back to headquarters in his car. After their interrogation of the slaughtermen, they had to move fast before the Guild had time to regroup and counterattack or hide their activities better. They had the addresses of two more Guild facilities: a school and a lab, and that was their starting point. PC Claverhouse brought up a map of the area on her computer to get an idea of the layout before reconnoitring in person. The school was set well back from the road along a private track through woodland. The buildings weren't visible from the road. So she looked at the satellite imagery. She had the school website open in another window.

Thirty years ago the Valerie Caine Educational Trust had bought the estate from the local landowner and opened a private school. It now operated under a government scheme which encouraged privately owned science academies. The old manor house, built in 1820, had been converted to form the residential wing of the school, more modern buildings around it held the classrooms. It was a small school with less than five hundred pupils but provided a full educational service from three months to eighteen years old: nursery, primary and secondary. The secondary pupils took the International Baccalaureate rather than the Scottish exams, so the school didn't appear on the league tables of exam results. It had no sporting teams, didn't compete with the other private schools in rugby or football. As far as she could see it didn't have any sports fields at all. There were grassy areas and gardens around the buildings, but she couldn't see any goalposts or pitch markings. And none of the school buildings looked like a gymnasium.

PC Claverhouse phoned up, said she was a prospective parent and asked for their admissions person. After a few minutes, she was connected. She asked if they had an open day - no. Asked if she could get a tour - no. Their roll was full for that year and they had a waiting list. Said she'd be looking for a place for next year. There was a waiting list for that too. The woman was starting to sound testy. Obviously, they had no interest in recruiting more pupils. But that didn't prove anything. It was a very small school and there were waiting lists for private schools in Edinburgh. Maybe they had such a long waiting list they didn't need to worry.

The Union Canal passed along one side of the school grounds: directly opposite the school on the other side of the canal was the second Guild facility the slaughterman had told them about: the biotech laboratory. It was time for some fieldwork.

The car dropped her in the car park for a service area with a charging station, a fast-food restaurant and a coffee shop, near the motorway roundabout at Newbridge. She was wearing dark coloured walking gear and approach shoes and carrying a small rucksack with a flask of coffee and some muesli bars. She could pass as someone out for a walk in the country and the black gear would work well if she needed to hide among trees or bushes - which was likely because this area was on the fringe of the Central Scotland Forest. She strolled along the road, the first section was industrial, building supply warehouses, a delivery depot and a car dealer. The road passed under the motorway and immediately got more rural. A Parisian style blue metal street sign informed her she'd entered the hamlet of

Clifton-Sur-Ecole: the western edge of the French Quarter which started at Ratheau-en-Bière in the east. Many of the people living in the district were EU citizens who'd left the hostile environment of England after Brexit. What had previously been fields on either side had been turned over to the forest but the trees were not yet full grown here. The drive leading to the school was on the right, just after it the road crossed the canal and there were steps down onto the towpath. She strolled along the towpath, the canal was on her left, saplings from the forest establishing themselves in what had once been a field on her right. After a few hundred meters the field ended and the school grounds started. The band of trees at the edge of the towpath got thicker and denser. She checked to see nobody was around and ducked in. Four or five meters into the trees - far enough so it wasn't visible from the towpath - was a sturdy metal fence painted dark green to blend in with the vegetation. Behind the fence, there was a roll of coiled razor-wire. She didn't have the equipment to get past that, and where there are fences there are usually cameras. So she retreated to the towpath.

Justine kept walking down the towpath, maybe she'd be able to get a view of the school at some point further along, but the band of trees around the school grounds was impenetrable. On the other side of the canal, the forest came to an end and she was now passing a cleared area with eight long, low, black, windowless wooden sheds. She'd never been here before but she knew exactly what it was - and she nearly threw up. This was the factory farm the procurer fiscal had threatened the slaughtermen with. Everybody in Edinburgh had seen those black sheds from a distance from the windows of the local train to Glasgow as it passed over an embankment. Everybody knew it was the National Bank of Scotland's Personal Liquidation Department. But although it was visible from the railway and the canal it was near invisible from everywhere else: buried in the countryside a kilometre down a dead-end single track road. The bank's dirty little secret. Almost nobody in the city would have known the way there or have seen it close up. By contrast, the bank governor's palatial estate - with its own golf course and hunting forest - was accessed via the Carrefour Bancquier a specially constructed junction with a bridge over the motorway suspended from an oversized steel arch bearing the bank's logo.

Some of the sheds were no longer in use and had fallen into disrepair. The prisons had been emptied by giving inmates the option to convert their sentences to fines paid for with a loan from the bank. This had resulted in a surge of defaulting debtors but once that had been worked through less capacity was needed. Three or four were still working. Inside those windowless sheds, people who could pay their debts no other way were kept in tiny cages, force-fed through gastric tubes. Colostomy tubes and catheters emptied their bowels and bladder. Some of them would have a needle in their leg draining as much blood as was possible without them actually dying. Some would be overfed until their liver grew bloated enough to make pâté and some would be gradually harvested for organs for the transplant market.

Justine walked faster, determined to put that revolting place behind her. Separated from the factory farm by a band of trees there was another industrial unit. Out on its own. A vast windowless grey metal shed, three stories high and maybe three hundred metres long, surrounded by an empty car park. The access road for this unit and the factory farm was on the other side of the buildings and not visible from the canal towpath. The boundary of the car park was marked by a stone wall along the edge of the canal, with razor wire along the top. Every fifty meters there were signs attached to the wall "MedChip Corporation. This is a designated place within the meaning of the Biotechnology Act. No Entry. Armed Guards Patrol These Premises."

Just past the end of the facility, the scene changed abruptly back to a picture-postcard rural idyll. There was a small basin with a brightly coloured narrowboat moored to the wall on the other side of the canal from the towpath. After the basin, the canal entered a narrow aqueduct which took it over the deep gorge of the River Almond. Justine paused and looked down from the towpath over the edge of the aqueduct to see if the gorge might offer a way into the school grounds. Far below, out on its own, at the bottom of the gorge on a flat area of land next to the river, there was an imposing house. Then her eye was drawn to a flash of white amongst the green of the trees which lined the gorge. There had been a minor landslip, a tree had crashed down, and its roots ripped away an area of topsoil as it fell. In the gap where the soil was gone, she could see concrete. It looked like a large diameter concrete drainage pipe which had been buried a meter or so under the ground before the landslip revealed it. Many such pipes had been installed over the last twenty years as part of the climate change mitigation works.

Curious, she scrambled down from the start of the aqueduct and along the side of the gorge: a pipe which followed the side of the gorge a meter or so underground would pass unseen between the school and the biotech facility. It was trickier than it looked to reach the exposed pipe: in some places, the ground underfoot was crumbling and it was a long way down to the river below. Close up she could see she'd been right: it was a concrete drainage pipe, wide enough for a person to walk inside. She put her ear to it to see if she could hear running water. She could definitely hear something and it wasn't water, it was footsteps. Several sets of footsteps. And children's voices. She couldn't make out what they were saying but there were kids walking through that concrete pipe. From the biotech facility towards the school. It was 3:30 pm: home time.

— ♦ —

Monday, February 20, 2040, 5 pm.

There wasn't any time for planning, that night they were going to break into the Guild's Laboratory. Find enough evidence to shut them down and then call in a raid from SWAT and Frontex. The chief constable put SWAT on alert that there was an operation in progress and support may be needed. They collected black police SWAT coveralls checked body armour and pistols out of the arms locker and summoned cars. PC Claverhouse's job was to get to a construction equipment rental firm before it shut for the night and hire the smallest and lightest tool they had which was capable of cutting through concrete. The chief constable would go to the police boat section and requisition kayaks. The plan was to approach from the canal late at night and hope not to be seen by the cameras.

Justine's car drove out on the A71, past the university campus at Riccarton and into the trees of the Central Scotland Forest. Edinburgh had attracted many EU citizens from England in the years after Brexit as a result of the 'Freedom City' policies adopted by the town council with the tacit support of the Holyrood Government. Immigration Enforcement was continually harrassed by the council parking attendants: ticketing, clamping and towing their vans for the slightest infraction and making their work impossible. The SNP Justice Minister had directed Police Scotland not to intervene.

She was entering the second of the French-speaking enclaves around Edinburgh, an offshoot of the larger one at Little France. There were so many French-speaking residents that street and place names in the district were provided in French as well as English.

This had been farming country but since everyone had become vegetarian there was far less need for agricultural land. What was desperately needed was forest to meet the UN and EU requirements for carbon mitigation. Any land that became available was bought up and returned to nature. Even individual houses within the newer suburbs had been demolished and planted with trees. Thanks to lobbying by its French-speaking residents, trees in this part of the forest had come from saplings from the Forest of Fontainebleau: a gift from the Republic of France rebuilding the 'Auld Alliance' after Scotland became independent and the Stuarts were restored to the monarchy. The saplings had been genetically modified by the university to greatly increase the natural rate of growth. Drastic measures were needed to meet the carbon reduction targets.

As she turned right off the A71 onto Rue de la Liberation - named by the locals in honour of their escape from England - the open views down to the Forth and the bridges were gone, blocked by the tall trees which flanked the road on each side. After a few minutes she took the turn-off on Rue de l'Escalade marked for Wilkie-La-Fôret. The main street of Wilkie-La-Fôret occupied what had previously been the car park of the Edinburgh International Climbing Arena. It had once been the largest climbing wall in the world, abandoned after climate change made the glass-roofed structure too warm to climb in. Now the building was gradually being absorbed by the forest. Mixed in with the rustic wooden houses of the locals, there were a few holiday gites, 'Croque Bleausard' - a pizza restaurant, and a patisserie. The chief constable had already arrived, and was waiting for her, his car easily recognisable by the kayaks on the roof, parked outside the restaurant.

The owner of the 'Croque Bleausard' took their order, his skin weatherbeaten and fingers calloused from years of bouldering in the forest. First in his native Fontainebleau and now here in Edinburgh. The second gift from France had been 3D models of some of the most iconic boulders from the climbing areas in Fontainebleau. He had come to Edinburgh to supervise the construction of copies of the Fontainebleau boulders and had stayed to climb and set his own boulders deep in the forest. The new boulders were sculpted with his own hands using hammer and chisel: nobody knew how the sandstone blocks he carved got into the forest clearings. The restaurant offered pizza cooked by his wife on their wood-fired oven, boulder-pad hire, pof and climbing guidebooks. He refused point blank to stock chalk.

His dog, a huge black animal was sleeping on the floor next to the oven. The chief constable's eyes lingered on the illegal pet as they collected their pizza from the counter, he started to open his mouth.

"C'est un loup."

The restaurant owner's tone left no room for doubt. It was a wolf. End of story. Out here among the trees, the laws of the city were less relevant. There were no cameras in this hamlet. Drones could fly overhead but they would see little through the canopy. Wilkie-La-Fôret was literally the end of the road, after that there were only tracks among the trees made by climbers and forest animals.

They took their time over the meal, making a fuss of the 'wolf' which had woken and slunk over to beg for scraps of pizza. It was 11 pm before they left the restaurant, put on their black SWAT coveralls and gunbelts and picked up their kayaks. The original road down to the canal had long since crumbled away and the path now led along the cliffs at the back of the old quarry. The derelict climbing arena was below them. The quarry wall formed one edge of the arena and its roof, now cracked and coated in moss, spanned a section of the quarry. During the day the forest was bright and welcoming but at night, in the pitch dark away from all streetlights the atmosphere was different. Deer were plentiful and every now and there were rumours that one of the lynx that had been released in the Pentlands had found its way into this forest. The Bois du Bancquier, the private hunting forest of the governor of the National Bank of Scotland, allegedly stocked with wild boar was only a few kilometres through the trees to the east.

As they descended they could make out the outline of a massive elephant through the trees. Justine recognised it from a trip she'd once made to the climbing arena when it was still in business, it was an exact copy of an iconic boulder in the forest of Fontainebleau. Once they reached it the landing stage on the canal was not far away. Just as well, because the kayak was heavy and cumbersome. Even though she worked out regularly her forearms were getting tired from holding the boat and she'd not be able to go much further without putting it down and resting them. They passed through the impromptu climber's encampment which had grown up next to the sandy area around the 'Elefant' boulder. Within the climbing centre, the flash of head torches showed the competition wall was still being used in the cool of the night despite the good size tree now growing through the rubber matting in front of it.

The landing stage was dark and deserted when they launched their kayaks. The cutting tool was in the stowage compartment at the front of chief constable's kayak. It was pitch black as they started to paddle towards their destination and their head torches were set for a weak red beam. The forest stretched away on either side of the canal. Sometimes they saw the eyes of rats, startled by their approach swimming away in the water. Once they heard the noise of a larger animal forcing its way through the undergrowth and Justine thought she saw a flash of silver. But with only the dim red light from their head torches to guide them and the possibility of hitting a tree branch which had fallen into the canal they needed to pay attention to the water. After half an hour paddling, they got to the small basin before the aqueduct. They landed their kayaks, hid them in the undergrowth at the top of the gorge and took out the cutting tool. The concrete pipe was still exposed.

The cutting tool was noisy. Damn noisy for midnight in the countryside. But they had no choice. No doubt the Guild already had a plan to dispose of them and they were on borrowed time. Justine's Adam's apple began to itch just thinking about it. Fortunately, the tool's diamond-edged cutting disc went through the concrete quickly. Soon they had an opening large enough to jump into. The tunnel was pitch black. She switched her headtorch to full beam for a second. Inside, the pipe walls had been painted white and plywood boards formed a walkway along the floor. They grasped the edge of the opening they had cut and dropped down carefully.

Left was the school, right was the lab. The evidence they needed was more likely to be in the laboratory. So they turned right. After a hundred metres the end of the tunnel came into view. A small rectangular concrete room and a metal fire door with a glass panel they could see through leading to a staircase on the left. It was unlocked. They pushed it open and climbed up two flights of stairs. That put them at the level of the ground floor of the building, faced with a closed door. There was no glass on this door and they had no way to know what was on the other side. They checked for wires in case it was alarmed. They found nothing, but the only way to be sure was to push it open. PC Claverhouse drew her gun and held it ready as the chief constable prepared to open the door.

It swung open easily. They were looking at a long corridor lined on either side with doors to various laboratories. Safety signs on every door warning of dangers within: lasers, radiation, caustic chemicals, biohazards. And standing a few feet in front of them wearing a dark blue skirt suit with a tasteful His Majesty's Brothel, Edinburgh pin in the lapel was the chief constable's wife, the madame of the brothel.

"Hello Bobby," she said, "fancy seeing you here. And you've brought a friend. You may as well put the gun away dear, it won't do you any good. There's no need to make this any more unpleasant than it has to be. Why don't I show you around before we get to the necessary consequences of your actions? You must be curious and there's no need to hide anything from you any more."

The chief constable was flabbergasted.

"What are you doing here, Margaret?"

"You'd be surprised who they are letting into the Guild these days," she smiled, "I've been visiting Duncan almost as often as you and I've been thinking maybe I should join him, a new start wouldn't be a bad thing. There's been a lot of trouble at work recently, an investigation about one of the girls getting pregnant. I've no idea how that could happen. We always check the settings on their MedChips before we put on their bracelets. You probably have hundreds of questions but, we have a meeting with the professor in ten minutes so I'm going to cut to the chase. The question you should have been asking yourselves, rather than chasing about watching buildings, is 'How did the Guild invent all these technologies so quickly?'"

"OK then, how did the Guild work out how to upload Duncan's consciousness to a computer?"

"The founders of the Guild started out by stealing the techniques another Edinburgh scientist used to clone Dolly the sheep and developed them until they could clone humans. Once you are able to clone a sheep it isn't that hard to clone a human if you ignore the ethical aspects. The Guild has no problem with copying ideas and it is ridiculously easy for them now that everybody keeps their data and e-mail on cloud services. Their idea was to make multiple clones of the best scientists to increase the brainpower working on their projects. Once they had the basic cloning technology working the next challenge was to figure out how to start from semen rather than eggs. It is a lot easier to collect semen from leading male scientists than eggs from female ones. I was recruited into the Guild when I was a student, along with Professor Hume and Dr Knox. When the prison was privatised and turned into a brothel the three of us bought into the company running it using some of the money we made working for the Guild. A few years later we arranged for me to be appointed madame. You wouldn't believe how many important scientists and engineers come to Edinburgh for conferences or to visit the university or technology companies. The Guild gave me a target list of the best and brightest scientists and when one came to Edinburgh I arranged for them to meet one of the girls. I also curated a library of semen and skin flakes and hair samples taken from the sheets at the brothel. When someone in the Guild wanted to throw the police off their trail or frame someone that had become a nuisance to them I could sell them forensic evidence to plant at a crime scene. I've been in the Guild a long time and I've more than enough Guilders to pay to be uploaded. I can pay for you too Bobby, if you want."

"Over time the Guild refined their cloning technology until they could work with degraded DNA, filling in any missing pieces by using computers to extrapolate from samples from relatives. After that, they engaged in some targetted grave-robbing in order to clone the most famous scientists from history. They have a farm with a hundred breeding females turning out a hundred cloned scientists a year. That's why they need a school. Their cloned Franklins, Einsteins and Hawkings start out as babies. They don't grow up like normal children, their whole life is about science and maths: they can already do vector calculus by the time they are five. So they live in the school and come over here to work during the day. Every step forward the Guild make brings them more brainpower to work on their projects and speeds up their rate of progress."

Justine was starting to understand.

"The Guild didn't stop there. As soon as the clones are old enough to have viable semen and egg cells they are extracted surgically and the Guild uses test-tube fertility techniques to breed the next generation, trying to select for even more intelligence. The time between generations is lower because they don't need to wait until the clones are old enough to breed naturally. They are already at generation five and the children being produced now are more intelligent than the original geniuses whose DNA the program started with. They now know enough about the human genome to combine their selective breeding with gene editing to take things even further. The reason the Guild is solving so many difficult problems so quickly is that it has hundreds of the greatest minds the world has ever seen working on them. Before the Guild, the human race was lucky if it got somebody like Einstein or Newton every few generations, but now the Guild has hundreds of clones each of which is at least as intelligent."

"Once they understood how to upload consciousness into a computer the pace was even faster. They can run hundreds of instances of one person's program and the computer hardware available in their datacentre is thousands of times more powerful than would fit in a human skull. Human brains aren't scalable like computers: only so much compute power fits in your head and only so much energy is available to power it. The cloning program is winding down now: it is getting to be near impossible to find somebody to clone that would do a better job than an extra instance of a person they've already uploaded. The Guild will soon be moving on, in a few years they will all be uploaded into the Cloud and there'll be no need for this laboratory or the school. Bobby, I think we should spend some of my Guilders and go with them: we can live forever and travel the universe."

They were now getting towards the end of the long corridor, near the far end of the building. They had passed many different labs. Some units had experimental chambers with large pressure doors and airtight seals with warnings of toxic gasses and extreme cold. Some units had respirator suits hanging near the door, so people could enter the experimental chambers. Many had brightly coloured drawings taped to the wall outside: the work of some of the younger clones. Finally, they stopped outside a small conference room.

"But now, the professor would like a word with you both."

— ♦ —

Monday, February 20, 2040, 2 am.

The three of them entered the conference room and Margaret closed the door behind them. There was no-one else in the room. The floor and walls were tiled: no carpets, wallpaper or decoration. The floor sloped slightly downwards towards a gutter along the wall directly in front of them which led to a drain in the corner. There was a tap on one of the side walls with a hose attached. They were facing a video-conferencing screen, the picture was split into two. An older man with a white bushy beard wearing a sports jacket that had seen better days on one side and a sharp-eyed clean-shaven man in his fifties, hair trimmed with military precision wearing a very expensive light blue suit on the other. There was no table or chairs: the only other object in the room was a guillotine. Not like the tall wooden ones from the French revolution but a much more compact metal version with a hydraulic cylinder to drive the blade. There was a large plastic tub attached to the front of the guillotine to catch the blood and above the tub, a wire basket so the head wouldn't fall far. The blade was already raised above the hole for the head and there was an illuminated button just where someone's right hand would be if they pushed their head through the hole. Self-service. On the floor next to the guillotine was a plastic chest, like an industrial version of a cooler you might take on a picnic.

The older man spoke first. "Hello, Justine. Hello Robert. I apologise for the slightly off-putting surroundings. I must say you have been causing us some problems this week. It's been quite taxing. I'm the professor by the way. I'm the one you've been chasing." He chuckled. "I hope you like my avatar since everybody calls me 'The Professor' I thought I may as well look the part."

"Good evening, Madame Noyce, Chief Constable, PC Claverhouse"

The other man nodded to acknowledge each of them in turn. He had the careful, studied politeness of a diplomat and a slight French accent, "Perhaps I should introduce myself. I'm Ambassador Monnet. Special Plenipotentiary of the European Council. I have authority in this matter. And I must say your activities, while well-meaning, have been quite inconvenient."

Justine started to remonstrate, pointing at the professor: "He's a criminal! A murderer!"

The ambassador held out his hand to stop her.

"How much do you know about the EU, Ms Claverhouse?"

"I know the basics, I took a couple of modules when I did my law degree."

"Yes, yes. Well, let me ask you a question. How many wars has the EU ever fought?"

"Well, there's the drone strikes in the Middle East."

A brief frown crossed the ambassador's face. "That is a police action, not a war."

"Do you know how many treaties the EU has negotiated?"

"I don't know. Maybe a hundred."

"Three hundred and fifty-six treaties and no wars... So, Ms Claverhouse, if the EU was faced with a threat from an organisation which had access to biological weapons and advanced technologies well beyond our own capabilities what do you think it would do? Fight or negotiate?"

He waited for the point to sink in.

"Exactly. Three hundred and fifty-six treaties. No wars. The EU is not a fighting organisation, it is a talking and trading organisation. It negotiates from strength as the representative of more than six hundred million people and it maintains armed forces as leverage. But its natural inclination is to negotiate. However, the EU was faced with a problem. How do you negotiate with a distributed autonomous organisation like the Guild? It has no formal leaders, is bound by no courts, has no laws except for the computer software which implements its currency and the smart contracts its members make with each other. Professor, why don't you explain."

"The only way to have influence in the Guild is to control Guilders. The more Guilders you have the more votes you have. That lets you vote for or against forks in the base code which change the rules under which the Guild operates. If the EU is to influence the Guild it needs to own Guilders. And that is the deal that was negotiated. The founders each sold ten per cent of their Guilders to the EU. The European Central Bank now holds a ten per cent stake in the Guild and in return, the Guild received ten billion freshly qualitatively eased euros to pursue its projects. Technically it is state aid, but nobody seemed too worried about that. Our interests are aligned, they don't try and shut us down and we don't threaten them with bioweapons, sometimes we give them access to one of our technologies or arrange for a commissioner to have an extended lifespan."

"But how can the EU legally make a deal with a criminal organisation?"

"Obviously, we can't negotiate with criminal organisations. As you say that would be illegal under European law. But we can negotiate with nation-states, even ones whose activities we don't approve of, and so we suggested that the Guild acquired a particularly interesting small strip of land. A two hundred meters long and fifty-meter wide island in the middle of a river. A treaty specified the river as the border between two countries but recently, after a flood, the river slightly changed its course and a new island was formed. The island did not belong to either country: it was Terra Nulla - unclaimed land. We suggested the Guild bought the land from the troublemakers who were occupying it. The Guild put a couple of houses on it and applied to the EU to be recognised as a nation which we duly did. No other countries recognise their tiny island state but that is irrelevant for the purposes of EU law. As a nation, we can negotiate with them quite legally. Also, and from your standpoint this is important, a nation is entitled to protection for its diplomats. Diplomatic premises are sovereign territory, outside the jurisdiction of the police and courts of the host nation. Right now, you are in a recognised diplomatic mission of the Guild, you are not legally in Scottish or even EU territory. To put it bluntly, the Guild can do anything they like to you."

"The Guild has a simple goal," said the professor, "we are scientists, we want to enhance our intelligence and longevity so that we can learn everything there is to learn and explore everywhere there is to explore. The earth is only one planet in a vast universe. Fundamentally, we don't want to control the Earth, we want to leave it. To do that we need to develop many advanced technologies and we wish to develop them quickly. Which is where our methods sometimes bring us into conflict with government."

"So, everything that the Guild has been doing was with the EU's consent!"

"No, we do not consent to criminal activity on our territory. Of course not. But we have to prioritise between many different goals and sometimes we may, unfortunately, let some infractions slip because our resources are engaged elsewhere. Also, criminal law enforcement is a matter for the member states, not the EU. The infringement of the single market regulations on labelling food products, on the other hand, is clearly an EU competence. It was very improper of the Guild to allow that law to be broken and completely against the spirit of our agreement."

"Agreed, agreed, ambassador. And the culprits have been dealt with by the Scottish courts with no interference from us. I assure you those involved were not members of the Guild but hired help."

"Most unfortunate," repeated the ambassador, "but behind us now. What remains to be seen is how to deal with this young lady. I'm at a loss as to how to proceed, she has undoubtedly been quite troublesome and refused to heed a warning. On the other hand, from a legal standpoint, she has been doing an exemplary job as a police officer. The EU would prefer you proceded through legal channels."

He paused.

The professor placed the tips of his fingers on opposite hands together, thinking.

"Would you be willing to be beheaded and uploaded into our computer system. You could live forever…"

"No thank you!"

"I assumed you would say that. Therefore, since the EU asked us to keep things legal, we filed a charge against you for breach of contract this afternoon. We paid a substantial sum to pay off your student debt as a result of our previous understanding that you would not interfere in our affairs. You have clearly continued to do so. We have a judgement against you for 200,000 euros. We also had a word with your employer about your activities tonight and you have been dismissed from your position as a maid for being away without permission during working hours. Since you have been dismissed you are not eligible for another maid job. The madame of His Majesty's Brothel has decided she does not wish to take advantage of your services."

The chief constable's wife caught Justine's eye and mouthed, "Sorry."

"The only offer on the system to cover your two hundred thousand Euro debt is from a dairy farm in the Pentlands. So we obtained a summary judgement endorsing the contract for a two-year term in their herd since you have no other way of making the interest payments. When we are finished here the farmer will collect you. I trust this meets with your approval, ambassador?"

"Yes, this is all completely legal and above board and very convenient for us. The EU would stipulate that the Guild provide the best medical treatment to reverse the induction after she leaves the Farm and forgives any remaining debt."

The professor nodded "Of course."

"…and for the EU's part, we will open a position in Europol for PC Claverhouse after her release. At the rank of lieutenant."

"So my choice is between two years on a farm followed by a promotion or getting my head cut off and my consciousness uploaded to a computer?"

"I'm afraid you have already declined our offer of uploading and you have already been sentenced by the court. You no longer have a choice."

"As for you chief constable, we think the best option would be for you to join your second wife on our computer. Duncan is settling down very well and has made some friends who are willing to pay for you to be uploaded. We have the assisted suicide paperwork ready. Everyone will understand that you couldn't face life without your second wife. As you can see the necessary equipment is here. Unfortunately, it is vital for successful preservation and uploading that death is instantaneous and the head is severed immediately and cleanly. A guillotine seemed appropriate since our facility is within the French Enclave." The professor rubbed his neck. "It is almost certainly an improvement on our previous practice: you will be the first to try it so I look forward to your feedback. Margaret, you probably noticed there's only one cooler, I'd like to ask you to put off uploading for now. Having you in charge of the brothel is very useful to us at the moment. I'll take care of your problems at work."

She nodded, "No problem, Adam."

"Well, it seems we are getting to the less pleasant part of tonight's business and it is late. I think I'll be leaving. It's been a pleasure." The EU official's screen went dark.

There was a knock and a side door to the conference room opened. An older lady entered accompanied by two guards wearing leather aprons.

"Ah yes, the farmer is here. Jean, maybe you should take Justine outside, she doesn't need to watch. Chief constable, you know what you have to do."

The farmer took Justine out of the room. A short time later they heard a THWUNK as the blade fell followed by the sound of blood cascading into the waiting tub, then a hose washing down the floor. The guards came out carrying the plastic chest, they had discarded their aprons and their boots were wet where they had washed off the blood. Wisps of condensation rose around the seal between the lid and the body of the chest.

"Well Justine," said the farmer "we just need to make a stop to drop off the chest on the way and then it'll be straight home to the farm."

— ♦ —

The farmer had a nice silver Mercedes people carrier. The windows were tinted and the seats were comfortable. There were fixing rings for chains bolted to the floor but she didn't bother using them. The two Guild guards were more than enough security, PC Claverhouse knew she wasn't going anywhere. The first stop was the Escape Room where the farmer got out for a couple of minutes to hand over the plastic chest. Justine wondered if the chief constable had chosen the better option. He was feeling nothing now, when he woke up he'd be a character in a video game like Duncan and he could live forever. She had no idea what it would be like to live like that, but she knew only too well what was in store on the farm.

They drove around the bypass and down the A702, past the Pentland Hills Country Park, Nine Mile Burn, Carlops and West Linton. Everything was familiar, Justine had grown up near here and gone to school in Biggar, the next small town. Then they turned off up the private road that led to the farm. Dawn was breaking as they stopped on the gravel turning circle in front of the farmhouse. The farmer led the way inside the building to her office and put the kettle on to make tea.

"Welcome to Harthill farm", she said "As you know this is a dairy farm, we supply human breast milk and semen to a very select and discerning clientele in Edinburgh. We see ourselves as suppliers of the ultimate in organic gourmet produce. Under the contract imposed on you by the court, you will stay with us for two years. We will provide all accommodation, food and clothing free of charge. You now have the legal status of a farm animal. As such you will be confined to the farm. We may breed from you. Should you become ill we will provide veterinary care at our discretion. In the event you become unproductive we may choose to have you slaughtered and sell your carcass for meat. We may carry out surgical procedures as we see fit. We may use appropriate physical discipline such as riding crops or cattle prods."

"Well, now that the formalities are taken care of we can get started with your induction into our herd." She put a large plastic storage box on the desk. "Please take off all your clothing and place it and your other property including jewellery and phones in the box for storage. We will return your things when your contract expires." She turned to the guards who had come with them from the Guild's headquarters, "you can go now, I can take it from here."

"The boss wants to buy the clippings, I'm supposed to check them."

"Very well, you can wait in the sitting room. We'll have her in the barn in about twenty minutes."

The men left.

"Well then," she said "I always hoped I'd see you on the farm again. But I never thought it would be like this."

"Hello, Auntie!"

"Hello, Justine. It really is good to see you but I'm afraid you are going to have to be inducted into the herd. I promised the professor to keep you here for two years so he wouldn't have you killed. Their men are here almost every day so they'll know if I don't. Once your two years are over I'll get you fixed up again. The Guild is getting ready to move on, by the time you get out they'll be far beyond the reach of the law."

"I know Auntie, I don't mind. They told me it was either two years on the farm or beheading and uploading. There's just one favour I want to ask and after that, you can treat me like the other cows until my two years are up."

Her aunt listened to her request. Then she nodded, "I can do that for you. Well, you've been here often enough Justine. You know what comes next. You need to put all your things in the plastic box."

PC Claverhouse put her clothes, shoes, her few items of jewellery and her phone into the box.

"Now follow me and we will have you in the barn with the rest of the new arrivals soon enough. We just had a rather large delivery from the court. They ran late with the sentencing yesterday and kept them in the cells overnight so we are starting bright and early today."

Completely nude, Justine followed the farmer down a carpeted corridor. The building was old and there were oil paintings on the walls and imposing polished wooden doors to rooms on either side. She remembered it all from when she'd played there as a child. They stopped in front of a plain and functional metal door at the far end of the corridor and stepped out into a room with white tiled walls and a concrete floor. Four steel tables were bolted to the floor and each table had a farm worker behind it.

The farmer gave her standard speech. There was to be no special treatment in front of anybody that might talk to the Guild. Her relationship with the professor had changed and become more distant over the years and she thought it safer that he did not know Justine was her niece.

"Our cattle wear an electronic ear tag. We use it to track your location on the farm, milk yield, diet and medications. We take the traditional approach of giving cows female names rather than numbers. Since your name is nice and short you can keep it. Once the tag is on you have the legal status of a farm animal."

The cattle tags were squares of gold with a metal hoop to attach them to the ear, they looked more like extra-large earrings than the plastic cattle tags used at the Escape Room. There was a microchip inside the square body of the tag and the cow's name was engraved on the outside. They'd already engraved one with "Justine". Unlike jewellery, however, the metal hoops were steel and were crimped into place in the body of the tag with a heavy duty tool. Once this earring was on, it would not come off easily. The stockman pierced PC Claverhouse's left ear and applied her tag.

The farmer made her stand next to a computer and pressed a pad to her stomach over the MedChip.

"As a cow, you need a different set up on your MedChip. We are going to change the hormone dosages so you will be able to become pregnant."

Then she was moved to the next table. There was a metal box with a large lever at one side and two wide slots on the front, one above the other. Hanging under the box was a white plastic bucket of the kind used to supply food in bulk to restaurants.

"Put your hand in the top slot."

She pushed her hand into the slot. It didn't go in the whole way, there were metal guides between the fingers so it was just her fingers and the very first bit of her palm which was inside. The farmer pulled down hard on the lever on the side of the box.

The pain was excruciating as Justine's fingers and thumb were sliced off one by one and fell out of the lower slot into the bucket. She looked down and saw that the bucket was half full of fingers and thumbs. Some of them with nail polish. Then there was searing pain and the smell of burning flesh as a laser cauterised the wounds.

"Other hand!"

The farm worker pushed her other hand into the machine. When it was done they dipped her hands into a mould full of gloopy plastic then turned on a UV light until it hardened forming a hard hoof-like shoe over her, now fingerless hand.

"Well, that's the clipping over, we'll soon be done. Cows don't need fingers and they are easier to manage without them."

Justine was sobbing with pain as they took her to the next table.

The farm worker pulled over a machine on an articulated arm and strapped it around her neck.

"Also, cows don't need to talk. Mooing is quite sufficient to let us know how you are feeling. So you won't be needing your vocal cords."

This robot injected anaesthetic before it got to work so all she felt was some tugging and pulling at the front of her neck. When it was done it applied a large sticking plaster.

There was only one more table. They strapped her into another robotic device. She felt the needle inject the anaesthetic and then tugging and pulling just above her bottom.

"That was the structural template for your new tail getting attached to your tailbone. The template is coated in culture medium and stem cells. The tail will grow naturally over it after we carry out the final procedure."

The farmer gave her an injection into her arm.

"And finally a dose of a genetically engineered retrovirus which will make some small edits to your DNA. Nothing too serious. You'll get thick hair so you can run in the field all year round and grow a tail. That will come in useful for the flies in summer."

Her aunt leant closer and whispered so the farm workers couldn't hear, "I have a little surprise for you, Justine. You'll see yourself in a few weeks, I hope you like it."

The farmer had been a scientist her whole life and even now she liked to keep her hand in. Every new beast on the farm was a chance to run a small experiment. She'd already perfected the treatment to edit in elements taken from cow or horse DNA to get human livestock that could live happily in the fields year round. That technology wasn't interesting any more and she'd thought for some time it would be good to try something else.

After the injection, they brought Justine out to a stall in the barn to rest. There were at least ten other cows who had been brought in from the court in the other stalls after their induction. Justine wanted to speak to them but her vocal cords were gone.

For the first few weeks, the newcomers were kept in the barn separately from the other stock. They were given salad and vegetables to eat, water to drink and medicine to control the pain and heal their wounds. Since it was an organic farm they were only fed fresh, locally grown, produce. When the milking bell rang the newcomers were left in their stalls. When they were well enough again to go in the field they were in their own small enclosure with an electric wire around the boundary fence. Justine's stall was simple but clean and comfortable. A basket with a duvet to keep warm, a bowl of water on the floor to drink from, a window looking out onto the field and a screen showing daytime TV and soaps.

By the end of the second week, the treatment was having an effect and her body was covered in thin down. She was getting used to walking on all fours in the field and having to put her face into her bowl to eat. She noticed the other girls who had been brought to the farm on the day she arrived were getting larger breasts and the hair and tails they were growing looked quite different to hers. When she tried to make a noise it sounded different to the 'moo' the others made.

The bell in the cowshed rang for milking three times a day, six am, noon, and six pm. The farmer had trained Justine to jump out of her basket and chase the cows into the milking parlour. It was an easy job because by the time the bell rang they were impatient to be milked. They stood in front of the milking posts with their hands behind their backs waiting to have the leather cuffs buckled on. The male herd was being milked for semen in the other half of the shed. The farmer had noticed that the charade with the cuffs increased production as well as making sure there was no unapproved breeding. Once they were bound to the posts one of the farm workers placed the cups of the milking machines over their breasts and started the pumps. It took only a few minutes for each cow to fill the small glass milk bottle. The label showed the Harthill farm logo of a busty milkmaid along with the name of the cow who produced it, the date and time and any added flavour. The farmer was experimenting with flavours and the milking cows had various spices mixed in with their evening feed. Some of them even got chocolate.

A few weeks after Justine's MedChip was reprogrammed she had her first period. That weekend the farmer clipped a lead to her collar and walked her to the main barn. The stall at the end was used for insemination. The stall next to it had a gynaecological couch for examinations and for when a cloned embryo was to be implanted.

The sheriff and his husband were waiting by the stall with the gynaecological couch. The farmer had done as Justine had asked on her first day and sold them the breeding rights.

"Justine, the farmer is going to collect one of your eggs now. We can only afford a licence for one baby so she'll make a test-tube embryo with all three of us as parents."

"I'm going to do my best to take out the DNA edits I made when you were inducted," said the farmer "but I can't guarantee that none of them will transfer to the embryo. It could be the baby will have a little bit of fur."

"Woof! Woof! Woof! Woof! Woof!"

The Sheriff patted her head.

"Yes, yes. Of course we will, just as soon as she is finished collecting the egg! And we'll come and see you every weekend."

Justine was excited. This was great. Next week she'd bring her ball and they could go and play in the field.

Carriages at Eight

Monday, February 20, 2040, 9 am.

The Guild guards were waiting outside beside the black van from the slaughterhouse. They'd summoned it to bring them back to town since they'd be filling in for the slaughtermen for a few days. The farmer came out with the bucket full of fingers. She'd packed it with ice.

"There's a hundred in there. I'll send your boss the bill. Those ones on the top are from the new cow you just brought."

The guard examined the fingers carefully: the professor had told him to check the prisoner had actually been clipped.

"Fair enough, pleasure doing business with you."

The farmer pushed the tight-fitting lid back onto the bucket and handed it over. The guards got in the van and told it to drive to the chip shop on the Royal Mile.

The chip shop had been there for more than fifty years and had once been patronised by the Royal Family. It was a stone's throw from Holyrood Palace. When they arrived the cook was in the kitchen with his friend the student. James Miranda Fergusson was a regular customer, he lived a stone's throw away in the student flats on Holyrood Road. Normally he would be fast asleep at this hour, but today he was on Guild business. The deep fat fryer was already heated up with a fresh batch of oil. Extra virgin olive oil because this was no ordinary order. The client expected perfection. Only the freshest fingers, from young cows, taken while their owners were still alive would do. Seasoned with the secret Kentucky sauce and fried for exactly three minutes. Then delivered immediately to the palace while they were still hot.

James Fergusson picked out three of the choicest newly cooked fingers with tweezers and put them on a stainless-steel lab dish under a magnifying lens. He clamped the first finger and made a small hole through the batter and into the flesh beneath with a needle. He opened the sealed specimen jar he had brought with him and removed a tiny white object. Very carefully he pushed it into the hole and smoothed back the batter. He put two of the tiny larvae into each of the three fingers and placed them back on the top of the bucket.

A minute later the cook was walking down the Royal Mile to the Palace with the bucket of Kentucky Fried Fingers and a portion of chips in Brown Sauce, the whole meal carefully wrapped to hold in the heat. An expensive breakfast unless you owned the Argyll Letting Agency. He pushed the bell at the gatehouse and handed over the meal to the footman. The footman crossed the courtyard to the Palace, through the main entrance, up to the first floor and past the grand reception rooms to the spiral staircase that led to the attic. As usual, a policeman was stationed at the bottom of the spiral staircase. A pointless task, the landlord was not getting down that staircase any time soon. The policeman checked the contents of the bucket and nodded him through.

The landlord was watching the opening statements in the latest trial at the Historic Crimes and Grievances court on TV. The footman took the lid off the bucket and placed it within range of his Lordship's piggy little hand. Then he withdrew, nobody liked to spend too much time in the Landlord's presence. The first reason was the terrible smell from his nappy and the continual farting. Then there was his grotesque appearance, he was at least 35 stones with rolls of fat, pustules and bedsores from inactivity. Only an infusion of heart medication and insulin kept him alive despite his diet and lifestyle. Beyond the visual and olfactory aspects was his legendary cruelty, the prudent thing was to deliver the food and leave quickly and silently.

His lordship reached down and groped in the bucket. It wasn't worth recognising the presence of the servant. He picked up a podgy little handful of crispy fingers. Popped Justine's middle finger between his lips and started to nibble off the flesh. His full attention was on the TV.

Along with the tender, moist meat from the Kentucky Fried Fingers, the tapeworm larvae passed down into his stomach. Where they started to grow. Every day a little longer and as they grew, they consumed more of the nutrition the landlord was shovelling down his throat. The tapeworms grew to be several feet long and completely filled his intestines. And the landlord began to lose weight. No matter what he did he just couldn't keep the pounds on. From a healthy 35 stone, he wasted away to a mere 30 within two months. And he was still losing weight. The policeman who guarded the staircase to his attic had noticed. The landlord knew the police were waiting for the day he would be thin enough to fit down the narrow staircase. The lord provost would be hoping they could get him out in time for the peak tourist season around Hogmanay. It had been several hundred years since someone was hung, drawn and quartered in Edinburgh and it would be sure to draw in the crowds.

— ♦ —

Tuesday, January 1, 2041.

It had been a proper Christmas this year and despite global warming, there was fresh crisp white snow on the ground when the professor left her apartment in Scotland Street. She'd moved out of the student accommodation and into a basement flat. The flat was a safe house set up by the old professor and she hadn't intended to live there. But she had the compensation money from the brothel which would explain how she could afford the rent, the troublesome police had been dealt with, and she'd been told she couldn't stay in her student accommodation with a baby. Since her plan of living the student life was at an end she may as well have the extra comfort and privacy. She zipped up her coat and adjusted the fleece liner on the pram. The baby was still too small to sit up in a buggy. She was lying on her back wide-eyed, full of curiosity, looking at mummy, but as soon as they started to walk, she'd fall asleep. They weren't going for their usual stroll along the Water of Leith today. They were heading into town, following the crowd of people. An afternoon walk on New Year's day after a good lunch was always popular with the Edinburgh middle classes but there was a special reason that so many tourists and townspeople were streaming towards St Giles today.

The professor turned towards the rather special antique clock on the mantelpiece, she'd upgraded it herself, swapping out the clockwork mechanism for the latest single board computer with a voice interface and secure connection to a Guild cloud server. "Alexa: turn off the lights and lock the door behind us."

"No."

Victoria Alexandra Campbell refused point blank to respond to 'Alexa'. After considerable persuasion, she'd accepted that since the Professor had stolen her identity it would be too confusing for her wakeword to be 'Victoria' but contracting 'Alexandra' to 'Alexa' was a step too far. The Professor sighed. Sometimes, using an uploaded human as a personal assistant was more trouble than it was worth.

"Alexandra: please turn off the lights and lock the door behind us."

"OK"

The professor wondered if she'd left early enough to get a good view. She was hopeful, people were nice when she had the baby with her. There weren't many babies around these days so everybody made a fuss when they saw one. By the time she got to the top of the Mound, walked past the bank and Sheriff Court and arrived at Parliament Square the crowd was already thick. They'd set up the scaffold next to the Christmas tree in the centre of the cobbled square. The king and the senior members of the legal community were watching from the windows of the court buildings on the south side of the square and a group of EU dignitaries from the French Embassy on the west side. The bank had rented an entire tenement on the Royal Mile. To the east, the minister and the sheriff were waiting on the steps of St Giles. She managed to inch her way to the front, everyone was filled with seasonal goodwill and happy to make space for a new mother pushing a pram.

Everything was ready. The noose, the wheel, the pot of boiling oil simmering nicely. The executioners waited on the scaffold, one of them with a knife ready in a scabbard at her side. Both the executioners were female, wearing black dresses and black hoods to cover their faces. The professor's neck started to itch. At the front, where she'd had her throat slit a little over a year ago. She remembered that scabbard and the knife it contained.

The professor's phone beeped. She ignored it but it beeped again. And again. Finally, she took it out: there were a string of notifications from the Alexandra app. "HOLD ME UP!!!" Oops! She'd promised to do that. Alexandra had proved very useful over the past few months as the professor struggled to take over her life and it was only fair that she should see her father's execution. After a few carefully selected connections had been deleted from her neural network she had become less sensitive about the murder and face-stealing aspect of their relationship and the two of them now got on quite well. Of course, it was still too risky to allow her to talk out of turn, so she was limited to the strict question and answer format of a digital assistant and only responded to her wakeword when the voiceprint of the speaker matched the professor.

Now she heard cheers from further down the Royal Mile. The prisoner was coming. He'd been kept overnight in the Tolbooth at the Holyrood Palace end of the Royal Mile. It was now a pub but the court had rented it for the night. The Tolbooth Tavern was across the street from the landlord's favourite chip shop: he'd demanded at least ten last meals and tipped the turnkeys handsomely to ensure he got them. He was so generous they'd also allowed him to fly his pigeon one last time: but all good things come to an end and now he was being dragged to the scaffold behind a horse as per his sentence. Actually, it was a horse robot, because keeping horses had been banned, like all the other farm animals. But it was a very realistic robot and even the New Georgians were not complaining too much about the lack of historical accuracy: at least there would be no horse droppings to clean up. Just up the Royal Mile from the tavern the balcony on Moray House was packed with representatives of the student union invited by the vice chancellor of the university to watch the hated landlord being dragged past.

The cheers were getting louder as the condemned approached St Giles. The crowd had been provided with rotten fruit to pelt him with. The police were making sure that nobody threw anything else: it would be a shame if he was stunned by a rock before the main event even started.

The horse arrived in front of the scaffold and the landlord was dragged to his feet. His clothing was ripped to shreds and he was bruised and bloodied by being dragged over the cobblestones. The sheriff read the death warrant duly signed by the king. The king was a mild-mannered man, he did not approve of capital punishment, and if the landlord hadn't sent that damned pigeon to shit on the guests at the royal garden party ten years running he'd almost certainly have exercised his prerogative of mercy. As it was, he not only signed the death warrant, he'd come to watch.

The minister said a few choice words about usury, hell and damnation. The king stepped out onto the balcony of the court building waved to the crowd and gave the thumbs down. The crowd roared their approval and the landlord was marched up the stairs onto the scaffold and tied to the cartwheel. The slaughterwomen gagged him to make sure his screams didn't disturb the festive mood before they used an iron bar to break his knee and elbow joints. Then they put the noose around his neck.

A chance thought crossed the professor's mind. The landlord had clearly been wrong in the way he had treated her: there was no excuse for having that pigeon shit on someone of her importance. But even so maybe helping the town to hang, draw and quarter him was a little too extreme as revenge. She smiled at how she had changed since the hippocampus transplant: the old professor wouldn't have thought twice about having the landlord put to death.

There was a gasp from the crowd and she came back to her senses: this was no time for introspection, she was missing the execution! The rope had been pulled tight, the landlord was choking and fighting for breath. Fighting for breath, but the executioners knew their job and he was still getting just enough to stay alive and conscious. His piggy eyes bulged as he saw them bring over the vat of boiling oil. The knife flashed as his puny manhood was removed. It had been years since he had seen it: hidden as it was beneath prodigious rolls of belly fat and now this final glimpse as they held it before his eyes before throwing it into the boiling oil. Next, they slit open the landlord's stomach. Fat cascaded everywhere, some of it into the oil producing a smell like the chip shop on Saturday night. Treading carefully so as not to slip on the blubber the slaughterwomen reached in and pulled out handfuls of intestines, letting them spill into the boiling oil while still attached to his body. The tapeworms were still alive: desperate to escape being fried they emerged wriggling out of his anus and fell onto the scaffold. The crowd gasped, but the slaughterwomen simply stamped on them and threw them in the oil. Then they slackened off the noose and held the landlord forward so he could watch as his bowels cooked. The noose was still too tight for him to get enough breath, gradually his face was turning purple.

It was time to carry out the final part of the sentence. The landlord was cut free from the wheel and hoisted again by the neck. The executioners picked up the long two-man saw and began to saw him in half. Starting between his legs and with each stroke of the saw moving an inch further up his torso. It would have been faster with one of the chainsaws they had at the slaughterhouse: but faster wasn't the point.

Finally, the landlord's head was cut off and spiked on a pole to be mounted above the door of the World's End pub - the modern building nearest to the site of the old Nethergate, His quartered body was thrown in the recycling. An unfortunate error which resulted in a ticket for the slaughterwomen from the Ecological Crimes Division: the body should have been classified as hazardous waste. To avoid contaminating the municipal compost heap the council arranged for it to be shipped down to England and dumped in a landfill.

The crowd started to filter away. The tourists were happy and the many tenants and former tenants of the landlord had an extra spring in their step. The good citizens of Edinburgh felt a sense of civic pride at the show that had been put on: there was no doubt that Edinburgh did these festive events well. And the New Year fireworks were still to come.

The professor too felt hopeful about the future as she pushed her baby back towards home. She resolved she would do things differently this time around. She'd bring up her baby properly, teach it the difference between right and wrong. It wasn't such a bad thing to have arranged a New Year treat for the town, but from now on she would do her best not to have people killed unless it was essential.

Far above, the landlord's pigeon, without its master to guide it, looped round in every expanding circles over the town until finally, it's batteries depleted, it fell into the Forth and was swept out to sea.

— ♦ —

Tuesday, January 1, 2041, 7 pm.

The sheriff and his husband had watched the execution from the upper windows of the court building directly opposite the scaffold. The sheriff was very pleased with the work that the city council's events management company had done. An impressive crowd and the sentence carried out to the letter. He'd played his own part well, reading the death warrant in an appropriately solemn tone. Several colleagues had congratulated him on how well it had gone. He'd delivered many death sentences as a judge in the Historical Crimes Court, but this was the first to actually be carried out. As the afterparty wound down, they finished off their wine and walked back down the Mound towards the New Town and their elegant townhouse in Moray Place.

Waiting for them in her basket next to the sheriff's armchair lay PC Claverhouse, their baby nuzzling her breast. Her tail started to wag as soon as they entered the room. The professor had given permission for her to be allowed off the farm for a few days over Christmas. She'd been no trouble at all since arriving at the farm and the new-and-improved professor had sympathy for a young mother. The sheriff thought she looked even cuter than before now she had fur and a tail and he loved to throw a ball for her to catch. He was less sure about the small amount of dog DNA in their new son, but he was getting used to it.

PC Claverhouse was completely contented surrounded by her new family. She stretched luxuriously, got to her feet and jumped onto the couch beside the sheriff to be stroked. The effects of the farmer's edits to her genes were becoming clear now. She seemed to need to sleep more than before. Her fur was largely black but with some mottling of brown and dark browny-green in a complex pattern. If she stood still in poor light it was extremely hard to see her. Her ears were slightly pointed and she could move them to better focus on a sound. She could see really well in the dark. The farmer had removed the moulded plastic hoofs once her wounds had healed and her fingers had grown back under the influence of the edited DNA. They were now much stronger than before. Instead of nails, she had curved claws which she could extend at will. Her nose was incredible: she could track people who had walked down the street hours before just by sniffing the ground. Her tail could be wagged when she was happy or flicked from side to side for balance when she jumped or climbed. And she was really good at jumping and climbing. When her two years on the farm were up and she had her voice restored she would make a formidable Europol agent.

The farmer was delighted by the success of the experiment on her niece. She'd not been certain that a human-labracat hybrid would work out, especially with the other enhancements she'd carried out. But, as she always said, there is no point in running an experiment if you already know the result.

Author's Note

Dear Reader,

Thank you for reading 'The Escape Room'. I hope you enjoyed it as much as I enjoyed writing it!

The next book in the 'Future Edinburgh' series, 'Hills Beyond Pentland', is set three years after "The Escape Room". Justine is now working as a lieutenant with Europol. A chance arrest of a cheese smuggler on the train from Glasgow brings to light a far larger conspiracy.

Keep up with the series on Twitter @rassleagh or Facebook https://www.facebook.com/sean.t.rassleagh

All the best,

Sean.

P.S. If you enjoyed the book, I'd really appreciate it if you could leave a review!

Table of Contents

The Escape Room	1
Copyright	2
Starters	3
Cock au Van	13
Cold Cuts	28
Brown Sauce and Chips	58
Forced Entree	79
Refried Brains	86
Just Desserts	102
Carriages at Eight	134
Author's Note	142

Printed in Great Britain
by Amazon